Secrets Unearthed
By Jennifer Brown

Acknowledgements
Cover Design by Sarah Fields
www.sarahsfields.com

I would like to thank those who have been supportive of my writing success. To the love of my life Bruce, for putting up with my ups and downs and still being there for me. I love you! I also thank my dad, Terry Brown and his wife Cari for letting me use their computer and printer when I needed it.

Chapter 1

August 16, 1992

Mark walked along the busy strip, his hands in his pockets. The night air was a little chilly, but he was anxious to get to his destination. He kicked an already broken beer bottle in his path as he trudged along the walk.

He gingerly fingered the bills he had in his pocket that he had just taken from the house guardian's wallet back at the group home. He hated the place. Most of all, he hated his father for sticking him there.

And····..if he was lucky enough to get his way····..he' d be out of there by tonight as well····.

Mark was totally unaware that he was being watched. And he had been, ever since he left. In fact, he' d been watched ever since he was dropped off at the teen group home.

The mysterious man with a ball cap and dark glasses watched from where he sat in his car across the street. He wanted so badly to be able to get out of that car now, run across the street and pick him up into his arms. It was so unfair to both of them that they had to live life like this.

But····..he had already checked into things and knew what he had to deal with. And he knew exactly what he had to do. He watched the boy until he knew he had to go, then he discreetly left the area····.

Mark barely noticed as the car slunk by him. Besides, he was almost to his destination. It was just up ahead.

He reached the front of the building and sat down. He must have been early. Of course, he did walk pretty fast. He had gotten a lot of practice

6

over recent years⋯.of running AND walking fast.

He laid his head against the brick front of the old building, waiting. He evidently fell asleep, for the next thing he knew he was being shaken by some guy he didn't recognize.

"You must be Mark," the guy said, once he had been startled enough into consciousness.

"Yeah," he answered, rubbing his head.

The guy then took a small bag out of his pocket. "I was told to bring this. Hurry up and hand over the money, I ain't got all day."

Without any questioning Mark gave him the money, and the exchange was made. The guy took off.

He gazed into the bag full of what looked like pencil shavings. He knew what it was though. He's been smoking it a little over a year now⋯ever since they left him in Hell⋯.

That night Mark opted to stay in an alley behind a dumpster. He used some paper he found to roll up the stuff and smoke it. He had borrowed matches from a drunk.

He lied back, smoking it, and already starting to feel much better.

"Hey Brewster⋯Thought I'd find you here."

He looked up to see his friend, as he sat

down beside him.

"I wish you'd stop calling me that."

His friend turned to him. "Why? It's your NAME."

Mark gave him a nasty look. "It is not."

His friend shook his head. "Ok….Tell yourself what you want. But we both know better, all right? You can't deny who you are. Look at me," he went on. "Daniel Scott Kirk, son of Camille and Scott Ryan Kirk…Stage actress and drunk."

Mark had no reply to that. He finished smoking his joint.

"So….What are you going to do?"

"What do you mean?" Mark asked, coughing.

"You know what I mean, Mark. You're free now. No house guardian, no nobody. You can go back to your mom and sister. You have to miss them."

Mark got up. "I'm starting to wish I had never confided in you," he said, walking off.

His friend yelled after him. "But you did Mark! Don't you think it's time? Time to admit to who you are and what you've done!? Grow up and accept it!"

Mark found himself on the other end of town at the park. He had amazed himself at how far and fast his legs could carry him. He found the shelter house and the bathroom, settling down to smoke another joint.

He had met his friend soon after he started getting the drugs. He had told him about his life, and urged him to tell him about his. Ever since he had regretted it. It was a part of his life he wished to forget. This was his life now, and he liked it. He liked being in control of when he would go to bed, where he'd take a piss or shit, and what he'd do in general.

He exhaled some smoke, closing his eyes and that's when he heard his voice again.

"Why do you keep running from me Mark? You know I'll find you every single time."

Mark winced.

"Come on Mark. You need to make a choice. You can't go on like this,"

"Why not?! I'm perfectly happy!" he protested.

"Well…. you're only 15. It's not too late to go back to your family. Your mother, your kid sister….Hell, you never really got the chance to be her big brother-"

The voice was interrupted as Mark got up screaming and charging towards the source of it. D.S. ducked though, laughing as Mark went into a high fit. He started banging the walls, and punching the mirrors, smacking them hard as they started to crack and red appeared on his hands from the broken mirror shards⋯.and he screamed out in agony⋯.

June 2006

　"Ahhhhh!!" Mark sat up, bolt upright in the bed. He sat there in bed, in a deep sweat as he fell back onto the pillow, closing his eyes trying to regain his breath. He heard a door open and opened his eyes to see a nurse standing over him.

　"Hey there hon⋯.you ok?" she asked.

　He gulped. Lying there, he began to remember everything that had happened. He had finally revealed the truth. Just as D.S. asked.

　Then he had saw the expression on his mother's face. Years of anguish came to the surface, years of anguish due to him. He had done the only thing he could do.

　He closed his eyes. "Is my mother ok?"

　There was a slight pause before the woman answered him. "Your mother is not your worry right now. You need to relax as much as possible."

　He looked at her. "What about my sister?"

　She took a deep breath, looking at him as if she were in debate whether to be honest with him or not. Honesty finally won out.

"Your sister has been here every day wishing to see you. Hon, we honestly didn' t think you were going to make it. You' ve been in a coma for three weeks. "

Meanwhile Elissa took a deep breath, standing backstage at The Tonight Show. She was just minutes away from going on to talk about her new movie which had been number one at the box office for three weeks, her Playboy shoot which had been done just last week and was already garnering a record number of pre sale orders, and last but not least···. her engagement to Kevin. It had already been made certain with the producers and the show' s host···. no questions about the events that unfolded three weeks ago. They had tried to keep it all quiet but it happened so quick. Everything just lost control.

She was pissed with Kevin about keeping the calls from her, the fact that she DID have a stalker···but she understood why he had done it. They ended up staying at the airport overnight in a secure location.

Greg had called her and told her what happened. D. S···..or as she now knew, her brother Mark···had shot himself right in front of their mother. Neither he or Kayla had been back to the house since it happened. But Kayla had opted to stay with a friend.

Elissa had come back to L.A. with Kevin, and Greg had come back with them which surprised her, considering another thing which was plaguing them all now, on top of everything else···. their father was missing.

"Ok···Thanks···..No, it's ok you're doing everything you can. Bye."

Greg hung his cell phone up in the other part of the room he stood in, backstage with his sister. He turned to glance over where she stood by the monitor, anxiously awaiting her cue to go on. He hesitated, setting the cell phone back in his pocket, going over behind her and putting his hands up to her shoulders.

He had pretty much taken over as Elissa's bodyguard. Kevin was busy signing a new movie deal that would basically set him up as one of the top ten bracket of movie producers, one of Hollywood's swankiest cliques.

She turned to look up at him. "No word on dad?" she asked.

Before he could answer though, the stagehand gave her a cue. She turned to approach the stage as they announced her···.

     Monica stood up gazing out the window of Greg's apartment. It was on the outskirts of their town. Greg had set her up with that, when she refused to go to L.A. with them. She couldn't go that far···not now. Not with her son lying in a hospital in a coma, and her husband missing. It was like a nightmare···. happening all over again.

     She went back over onto the sofa curling up on it and clutching her pillow. All she had right now was her daughter Kayla. And she wouldn't even stay with her. The last time she had been there was a few days ago, she stopped to see how she was, and borrowed twenty dollars from her. She was staying with Celia, her friend.

     Monica sighed, resting her head against the back of the sofa. That odd dizzy sick feeling she'd been experiencing for the past two weeks was returning. She didn't know what it was. She had gotten a pregnancy test to see if that could be it. At 47 she had not yet gone through menopause, it was still possible to concieve. Thankfully though, that had not been it. Monica lied down on the sofa, waiting for the odd feeling to pass···

His sister had been to see him. Mark blinked in astonishment. He had asked the woman if she could come in, and she said of course, that she'd been in there with him each day while he was unconscious. Of course…even if she DID come in…what did he say to her? She would think he was a total idiot, a mental nut…which he was.

He closed his eyes, suddenly feeling embarrassed and very vulnerable. Who was he kidding? He could never go back to that life and try to make up for what happened. The damage had already been done.

A soft, young feminine voice…not Elissa's…then spoke to him.

"Mark?"

He opened his eyes to see Kayla standing at the other end of the bed. He felt his heart immediately skip a beat. She was not who he expected to see. She stepped a little closer.

"It's Kayla…Do you remember me?"

Chapter 2

Greg stood backstage, watching on the monitor as his sister bantered back and forth with the show's host a forty something year old has been comedian. He did avoid bringing up the incident from three weeks ago. To make up for it, he teased her about her Playboy shoot, and Greg noticed a hint of disappointment in her voice when she talked about Kevin making his huge movie deal and having not spent much time with him lately. The host asked her about a recent snapshot of her and Greg at Starbucks earlier in the week, and she quickly explained Greg was her stepbrother, who was staying with her. After the host teased her about stealing her from Kevin, they went to commercial.

Greg's cell phone rang then, and he dug for it, answering.

"Hello?"

"Hey Greg…Elissa on yet?"

It was Kevin.

"Yeah, she is. As a matter of fact, they just went to commercial,"

"Great! I still have time to come there and

surprise her."

Greg blinked. "Surprise her?"

"Yeah···. Hey man, don' t breathe a word of this un il I get there, but I just signed the deal with Kriterion. The first movie I work on starts in two days and is being filmed fully in the Virgin Islands. I want to take Elissa too···. I think this is the perfect vacation we' ve both been waiting for."

Kayla gulped, trying to control her nerves upon going closer to him. Apparently she wasn' t as prepared for this as she thought.

He now looked, upon closer observation not so much like D. S. ···of course, she had been told he was wearing a wig and had contacts. He stared at her and it made her feel even more weird. Just as she was about to chicken out and turn around to leave, he spoke up.

"Yeah Kayla, I remember you. Have you been the one that' s been here everyday?"

During the commercial break Elissa talked a little more off camera to the host.

"How are things at home right now?" he

asked her out of what seemed like genuine concern.

She nodded. "Ok. I haven't talked much to anyone, I'm just trying to focus on other things right now."

He gave her an understanding smile as the stage manager warned them they had ten seconds before they came back to taping.

Greg stood there, still watching the monitor as the show's music started back up again. Kevin was on his way there, where he would break the news to Elissa about the Virgin Islands. Kevin hadn't mentioned a word about Greg coming, but he knew he'd be busy working and probably have hardly any time to spend with Elissa. They barely spent any time together now. In fact, in the last three weeks Greg had gotten to spend more time with his sister than he had since they were in school…. if not more. Everything which had happened, had made them grow closer.

"Hey Greg…. Ah, I see she's just about done,"

Greg turned to see where Kevin had stepped up beside him, gazing at the monitor with an excited smile on his face.

Kayla nodded. "Yeah, I've been here everyday."

He stared at her. "Why?" he asked, before he even realized he'd said it out loud.

She just shrugged. "Because you're my brother."

He gazed at her a while longer, eventually smiling. "Really?"

"Yeah···I mean, as soon as mom and Elissa told me about you, I refused to stop thinking about it or believe you were dead."

He gazed at her thoughtfully. "So···.what exactly did they tell you about me?"

She looked at him, and suddenly hung her head. He blinked, already having a feeling what they told her.

He closed his eyes for a moment, but then a thought struck him. Who was here for him? Who had wanted him? Who had believed he wasn't dead? Kayla. He could redeem himself through his youngest sister.

A smile then broke across his face. "Hey there···.Don't worry about whatever they told you," he went on, taking a deep breath. "Why don't you just let me explain myself to you?"

Elissa came backstage after the show was over and threw her arms around Kevin the moment she saw him. Greg just stood back watching them, as they kissed and then he broke the news to her. To say the least, she was excited.

"What do you say, we get out of here and celebrate? Greg you want to follow us over to Club H?" Kevin asked.

They each looked at him for an answer, but he shook his head···a little to his sister's dismay, he noticed.

"No, you two go ahead···I'm going back to the house···"

When Monica awoke it was pitch black out. She sat up groggily, rubbing her eyes.

What time was it? She was about to get up and go check and use the bathroom when the phone rang.

"Ohhhh," she moaned, walking over to answer it.

"Hello?" she mumbled tiredly into the phone.

"Hi Monica···I didn't wake you did I?" Greg's voice came over the other end of the phone.

"Oh..no, actually I just had a nap, dozed off," she went on. "What's up?"

"Well, actually a few things. Although

there's been no solid leads with dad, they have gotten a report of a man with his description going into a Bob Evans every morning in Bridgeport. They have someone following him to see what they come up with," he went on. "And···it looks like your daughter will be leaving soon with her fiancee for the Virgin Islands."

Once at the club Kevin and cappucino found a table and ordered drinks and appetizers.

"This deal has set me up Elissa. I now own some stock in Kriterion Pictures, I'm set up to produce at least ten movies in two years and our bank account has tripled. Not to mention all the perks." He went on. "This first vacation in the Virgin Islands is just one of MANY we'll get to take."

She gazed at him, with her chin in her hand. "It sounds positively fantastic."

"Yeah, and I know you need this and deserve it baby. Hell, we can even get married in the Virgin Islands if you want." He said, as their drinks arrived.

She gingerly sipped hers as he took several big gulps, his phone ringing . He picked it up, leaving her to mingle in her own thoughts. She had never been to the Virgin Islands. All this did sound great.

  She thought of her brother though. A part of her felt guilty for not being there with Mark, let alone her mother and sister but she had been busy. And Greg had been right by her side, despite things with Tom being missing.

  She closed her eyes, her mind and heart in turmoil. What the hell was she thinking? There was no way she could take a trip right now!

  Her thoughts were interrupted as Kevin shut his flip phone. "Ok⋯. Where were we?" he went on. "Oh yeah, that's right⋯So what do you think of a Virgin Islands wedding?"

Chapter 3

Kayla sat beside him, listening as he started from the beginning, telling her everything he'd been through. By the time he finished she still had her head hung.

He looked at her. "Hey, you ok?"

She bit her lip, looking up at him with watery eyes.

"Mark···. None of that was real," she went on. "The Doctor diagnosed you as a shizophrenic···"

Greg waited on the other end of the line for a response from Monica.

"Really?" she finally said, her voice cracking. "Must be nice."

He sighed. "I feel no need to go, but at the same time···." he trailed off, feeling helpless. "So um···how is Kayla?" he asked.

He heard a sniffle on her end. "I don't know. I haven't seen her in a while."

He blinked. "Do you think she's ok? Maybe I should call to check on her. What's her friends' number?"

He waited as Monica tiredly went to find Celia's phone number. He quickly jotted it down, and told Monica not to worry, he'd see to it everything worked out. He hung up with her and sighed rubbing his eyes.

"Where the hell are you dad? I don't know how long I can keep everyone together⋯."

After two more drinks, and three more phone calls to Kevin's phone, they headed home. Elissa sat back, gazing out the window. Kevin had spoken very little about anything else but Kriterion and frankly, Elissa was already tired of it. She hoped this trip to the Virgin Islands would help things between them.

They arrived back at the house, and Elissa went to the bathroom to take a long hot bath, jumping when she saw Greg standing over the toilet. She turned away.

"Oh⋯.God Greg, I'm sorry. I didn't know you were in here."

"I didn't even hear you guys come in. It's ok, turn around."

She did so, and he looked at her, as he flushed the toilet.

"So⋯you guys all set to go?"

She gazed at him. "Yeah, I guess. We leave this weekend."

He looked at her, concerned. "You ok?"

She blinked. "Well, yeah. It's the Virgin Islands! I could use a break."

Greg lightly smiled. "Is Mr. Big Time Producer even going to have time for you?"

She gave him a wry smile. "Even if he doesn't…It's still the Virgin Islands. I intend to enjoy every minute of it."

Kevin had gone directly to his computer getting on to confirm the flight for Elissa. Then he got to work on other finalizations with work. He wrestled his coat off, setting it on the back of the chair…not even noticing the message light on the desk phone blinking…

Mark lied there in the bed after Kayla had left.

They were calling him crazy. He had only half believed it over the years, that he was a nut case. Now he knew.

He hadn't said anything after she told him the truth. He was much too ashamed to. Now she was probably gone now too.

He closed his eyes, allowing tears to flow as he drifted off to another dream filled sleep⋯.

September 1993

Mark finished wiping down a table and picked up the two dollar tip the previous diner had left. He then picked up his tub, moving on to the next table.

He'd been lucky to get this job. He'd held it for three months. He was staying in a room a woman had rented to him above the diner. She was the wife of the guy who ran the diner, and took pity on him. He thought she liked him in another way too, from the looks she shot him.

He was 22 now, and still in the same town. D. S. still came to see him every now and then, but now he was more calmer. He acted as a true friend, which was what he needed.

He heard female giggling then, and turned to see a normal group of girls who came in every now and then. He never paid much attention to them since they were much younger, at least in their mid teens. But one of them liked to smile at him, and they all left huge messes with no tip.

Today they sat at their normal table, talking

excitedly about a dance at their school. Mark walked past them to set his tub down, and start wiping another table.

"Oh my God Christina! I can't believe you TOTALLY asked Greg out!"

"I KNOW! And he said yes. So⋯. Elissa, you should totally ask Brandon out. I know he likes you."

"No he doesn't. Besides, I don't even know if I can go to the dance or not. My mom's birthday is that night."

"So? Greg's going."

"Yeah, I know but he's just her stepson. Remember? My mom is no longer Monica Brewster, she's Monica Harner." she said, with a little disgust in her voice.

"Awwww⋯Elissa, why don't you admit it? You're jealous you can't have Greggy cause now he's your brother and not your boyfriend!" One of the other girls taunted her, but Mark was back at what Elissa had said.

He slowly turned to stare at her, this girl that had been coming in there off and on, realizing with a thundering in his heartbeat who she was. He shakily dropped his rag, turning to leave out the back door of the place⋯. never to return⋯.

June 2006

Elissa took a hot bath that night, lighting candles and turning on soft relaxing music. She put bath beads and bubbles in the water, and laid back relaxing.

She was so relaxed she didn't hear the door open and realize Kevin was in there, until he was in the water with her, gently caressing and kissing her. She felt enveloped by warmth, and sensuality letting him take every inch of her in. Next thing she knew, she felt him entering her and she gently and quietly cried out in ecstasy.

She gently wrapped her arms around his neck, kissing him as his manhood gently rocked her in the water…

Greg lied back in the guest room watching T.V. when, his cell phone rang. He quickly picked it up.

"Hello?"

"Greg? What's going on? I got your message." Kayla asked.

"Well, I was just worried about you. Mom said you hadn't been around much."

She sighed. "I'm fine. Please tell her not

to worry."

Greg blinked. "You sure?"

"Yes," she insisted, sounding a little annoyed.

"Ok," Greg said, picking up on it.

He hoped everything was ok, and that Kayla was just being a typical teen.

"Well…that's all I wanted. Are you ok with everything else money wise?"

"Yeah, I'm fine."

THAT was a shocker. Whenever he asked her if she could use some money, he usually got a totally different answer.

"Okay…. I guess there's nothing else to talk about then."

There was silence. Then she spoke again.

"How's Elissa? Have you hear from dad?"

Greg took a hand through his hair.

"Elissa's fine. As for dad…" he sighed, before finishing. Did he really want to get her hopes built up falsely? "…. No sis…. there's no word from dad."

Monica had lied back down, not feeling right. She wished her husband or at least Greg was there to take her to the hospital. Something wasn't right, she could feel it.

She drifted off, but was awoken by the phone the next morning. She sluggishly got up to answer it.

"Hello?"

To her surprise, it was Elissa.

"Hi mom. How are you?"

"Hi baby. I'm ok. Well…not great, but hanging in there. How about you? Greg tells me you're going on some big trip."

"Yeah, mom. That's why I was calling," she went on. "I…don't want to go unless I know at least you're ok…. so…. do you think I should go?"

October 1996

Downtown there was a huge Halloween party going on that night. Mark and D.S. Kirk walked through the throng, each dressed as skeletons.

"Where is she?" D.S. asked.

"It doesn't matter. I'm leaving as of tonight. Maggie gave me enough money to leave after I told her my story, why I couldn't stay."

"You're running away Mark. That's no answer to this."

"It is for me right now."

"Ok, so it is…. Where are you going?"

"As far away as I can from here." he answered him, going into the bus station up to the window.

"What's the next bus you have going through here?" he asked the attendant.

"I have one coming in about ten minutes, heading to Ohio."

"Ok, I'll take a ticket for that."

"Name?"

He bit his lip, turning to D.S. He had never given a name at the diner, for fear of being discovered. He was paid under the table.

D.S. slowly nodded, picking up what he was thinking as he turned back to the man at the window.

"My name's D.S. Kirk. Daniel Kirk," he said, suddenly feeling a lot better than he had in a   long   time….

Chapter   4

Greg was going to the kitchen and stopped outside of Elissa's and Kevin's room, overhearing Elissa's conversation.

"Well, yeah mom. Of course I want to go. It sounds truly amazing……. Are you sure? I just…… really worry about you." she went on. "I know mom. I miss you too. Bye."

Greg walked on towards the kitchen and grabbed a Mountain Dew. He took a drink, and let out a belch just as Elissa came in. He smiled.

"Excuse me…. I didn't realize you were coming in."

She went over and grabbed a bottled water from the fridge.

"I just called mom. I told her I didn't want to go on this trip with Kevin unless I knew she'd be ok."

Greg gazed at her. "And? What'd she say?"

She smiled, shrugging. "She told me I needed to go."

Greg looked down.

"I hate leaving you too though…with dad and everything," she went on. "Speaking of, you never did finish telling me about that."

He looked at her. He figured the same thing with her, as he did Kayla.

"There's no update on dad Elissa." he went on. "And⋯.don't worry about me. As long as I know you're happy and having fun, I'll be ok⋯"

Kayla entered Mark's room gently shutting the door behind her. He was asleep, but she could tell he was in a fitful rest. She stepped up to the side of the bed, drawing up a chair and sitting down as she tried to make out what he was mumbling.

"I'm D.S. Kir⋯⋯bus ticket to Ohio⋯"

She blinked. Ohio⋯..where he attended that school. Or so he said. They never really had the chance to check it out, everything happened so quickly. Now her father was gone, Greg and Elissa were back in L.A., and her mother⋯..she just wasn't the same. Nothing was.

Yet strangely she felt drawn to Mark⋯.He needed help and really, who else did he have at the moment? Who else did either one of them have?

Elissa went to bed without Kevin that night. He was still at work in his office. When she awoke the next day, she saw that the space beside her in the bed was still empty. In fact, it looked like it had never been slept in.

She sighed, getting up and going out to the kitchen⋯

Kevin remained in his office, zonked out with his computer still on alerting him to new messages. His head rested on his arm, which laid across the desk near the keyboard.

Suddenly, his phone rang, making him jump up awake. He wiped his mouth of some saliva that had dribbled out in his sleep, with the back of his hand as he reached to grab his phone.

"Kevin Lytle."

"Enjoy your partying last night? I've been trying to reach you."

He became more alert, hearing the voice of Randall Kitus, one of the heads of Kriterion on the other end.

"Actually I just went out for a drink with Elissa. I was working all night, and apparently fell asleep in my office."

Randall Kitus chuckled on his end. Thankfully, they had senses of humor.

"Well, that's good to hear you know how to balance things. I was calling to let you know,

33

details have been finalized. Your flight leaves
for the Virgin Islands tomorrow at seven. So be
ready."
    "Ch, I will. I'm anxious to get started on
this."
    "Just like we all are…." he continued.
 "So…. have you discussed what we brought up with
Elissa?"
    Kevin sighed, taking a hand through his hair.
 "Um…..Not yet. She's been through a lot,
Randall. I want to give her time to relax before I
bring something like that up to her."
    "Ok…Suit yourself, but she WAS part of the
deal Lytle. You promised us you'd get her."
    He bit his lip, nodding. "I know Randall.
And I won't let you down," he went on. "I
promise…"

    "Everything ok dear?" Celia's mother asked
Kayla as she sat at the table, slowly pushing food
around with her fork. She hung her head down,
staring at the contents of her plate. She didn't
even to hear her, and Celia and her mother both
exchanged worrisome glances.
    Celia gently nudged her friend.
    "Hey Kayla,"
    Kayla then looked at her.

"My mom just asked if you were ok."

Kayla turned to Celia's mother, her mouth dropping.

"Oh…..yeah, I'm sorry. I just…..I'm worried about my family."

Celia's mother nodded sympathetically. "I know hon. You know, my church has a few good youth counselors. I could call one of them for you."

Celia bit her lip, remaining quiet. Celia's mother looked at her daughter who just nodded knowingly at her, a silent way of telling her she would handle this with her friend. Her mother hesitated, starting to clear away the dishes.

Celia nudged her friend again.

"Come on…let's go to my room."

Greg didn't awake until much later, rolling over and adjusting his eyes to the bright sunlight which filtered throughout the room. He stretched before swinging his legs over the bed to get up. He walked over to the mirror in the room, gazing at his reflection before getting dressed in his khaki shorts and Hard Rock Café shirt. He remembered getting the shirt while he was with an old girlfriend of his. Pamela Stevenson. They dated for a week. Greg got tired of her bringing up Elissa every time she turned around. He had made the mistake of telling her they were related. He had wanted to impress her, because he liked her. Later on he discovered from a friend she was just a fan of Elissa's who already knew who he was. Ever since then, he hadn't bothered to date much. It was hard to tell whether the girl was dating him out of interest for him, or for Elissa. One of the downfalls of being related to a celebrity, he guessed.

He slipped on some tennis shoes, and paused before going out of the room. He noticed his cell phone had a missed call on it. He quickly picked it up to get the message that had been left.

Just as Kevin was hanging up with Randall Kitus, Elissa made her way in with a tray of mugs holding coffee and two bagels.

"Did you work all night?" she asked him.

He turned to her. Seeing the tray he appeared thankful and touched.

"Oh, hey baby. Yeah, I'm so sorry, I crashed in front of the computer," he said, laughing as she set the tray down. "I got some good news though. We leave in the morning at seven for the Virgin Islands."

Elissa looked at him wide eyed. "So soon? Good grief Kevin, I have so much to do…"

He shook his head. "Don't worry about it. I've already taken care of everything. I told you, it's time for you to relax and have a break. Let me do all the work," he said, taking a bite of his bagel.

Elissa sighed, folding her arms. "Well···I can't argue with the fact I need a break."

"Of course, you can't. So go ahead and get started packing if you want. Although, you don't have to pack much···.hell, with that expense account we can buy whatever we want once we get there,"

Elissa sat down sipping her coffee. She smiled at him.

"I can't believe we're actually going···.and so soon."

"Yeah, well···.Randall and them don't shit around either. They are on the ball and up front. They are why Kriterion is one of the best production companies out there," he went on. "And now that I'm a part of them···.Our life will never be the same."

When Mark opened his eyes, a doctor stood over him. He blinked several times, as if it hurt to look at him.

"Who are you?"

The doctor smiled. "Relax. I'm Dr. Torlan. Do you know your name? Remember anything?"

Mark took a breath. "Last I remember…I was hanging out with D. S. Is he here? Is he ok?"

The Doctor hesitated. "Yes Mark…He's fine."

Mark nodded, closing his eyes. "He's the best friend I've got right now. I don't know what I'd do without him."

Dr. Torlan folded his arms as he continued to interrogate Mark, in hopes to learn more where his mind stood. "So…you don't remember a young lady named Kayla? Or for that matter, Elissa?"

When he stated Elissa's name, Mark's face grew sharp.

"The second name I know. What about her?"

"It's ok Mark. Try to relax ok?" he went on. "Later today another doctor, Dr. Kellogg will come in to talk to you. He's a good colleage of mine and right now I think he'll be able to help you much more than me."

Mark shook his head. "Well, you never told me what was wrong to begin with," he said, a little in annoyance.

The doctor turned back to him before leaving the room.

"Let's just say…you have a lot to resolve from your past before you'll be mentally well

38

again···"

Monica paid the taxi driver before going into the hospital. She made her way up to the registration desk, waiting until the woman there got off the phone to attend to her.

"May I help you?"

"I'm Monica Harner, and···I just don't feel right. I need to be checked."

"Ok", the woman said, handing her a clip board with a few forms attached to it and a pen. "Go ahead and fill this out and just bring it back when you're done."

Monica nodded, taking it and going over to sit down a long one wall of the waiting room. It was moderately busy with a few guys waiting as well as an older woman and a couple with a baby. Monica shakily started filling out the information, hoping Greg received her message.

Greg listened to her message, as his heartbeat quickened. Monica was not feeling good. She was going to the hospital, and she hated to ask but she did, sounding very close to tears in the process, if he could come there. She needed someone and right then Greg realized it had to be him since his father was still missing.

He took a deep breath, dialing the airport's number to get the next flight back to St. Louis.

Chapter 5

    Once up in the room, Celia managed to get it out of Kayla what was bugging her. She broke down and told her everything and begged her not to tell anyone else she had even been going to see Mark.

    "It's ok Kayla. I already knew you were going to see him."

    Kayla stared at her. "How? Did you follow me?"

    She shook her head. "No, mom has a friend who works at the hospital and saw you. We all knew, and you really don't have to be ashamed or upset. After all, he IS your brother, you have every right to see him."

    Kayla wiped her eyes, resting her chin in her hands. "I wish I knew why I felt so drawn to see him so much. I mean, it's not like I never had a brother before. I have Greg."

    Celia smiled. "Maybe just because it's been hidden from you for so long···and he's a writer···who sort of wrote about your family, no less···"

    Kayla looked back at her hopefully. "You think so? That would make sense,"

"Yeah. What else could it possibly be? Kayla you can't analyze everything. It will drive you crazy."

Kayla blinked, realizing logically thinking she was right. She took a deep relaxing breath. "Maybe···. I need to stay away from there for a few days. He really scared me today."

Celia nodded, tucking her feet underneath her on the bed, Indian style. "Yeah. I think that's a good idea." she went on. "And we can hang out a little more···"

A little while later Mark had zonked out once again after a nurse came in to give him some medicine. He lied there in a restful sleep, not even awaking at a little past two in the morning when someone else, wearing a hospital uniform entered his room. Only a faint light, used as a night light shone right next to the bed, as the person stepped up beside Mark, wearing rubber gloves as they inserted another tube into his IV.

Mark's death was quick and painless. The person then stuck the old tube in their pocket, then in an odd move, pulled the sheet up closer to Mark's chin, as if they were tucking him in.

"Rest in peace Mark···" the male voice went on. "This is the best thing right now for everyone…now, I'm off to Paradise to end this once and for all…."

Chapter 6

Greg had a flight out that night.

Now all he had to do was debate on what to tell Elissa. He didn't want to alarm her…but he thought she should know about her mother. He decided to make it out as what it was. She wasn't feeling well, but right now it wasn't serious…and she wanted someone with her.

"Greg…hey, I'm glad you're here. I guess…we're learning a little earlier than we expected."

Greg turned to see Elissa as she came in the room, with an expression that told him, she anticipated his reaction.

"Oh, really? Well…I'm heading out tonight myself."

She gave him a surprised look. "Really? Where to?"

He looked down. "I'm going back home. I feel like I should be back there with your mom and Kayla. Besides she called me earlier, asking if I could come back."

"Is she ok?"

"She's fine, sis. Don't worry." he went on. "In fact, I'll probably be gone before you."

She stood there, staring at him. "We leave in the morning. Will you at least let me take you to the airport?

He smiled. "I don't see how I can refuse⋯"

Monica sat in the examining room, nervously awaiting to see the doctor. A few nurses recognized her, and asked how she was and if she had heard from Tom. She could only shake her head. She felt so dizzy⋯. and sick.

"Hi Monica."

She looked up to see one of her husband's good friends and colleagues there, Dr. Romano.

"Hi⋯You're actually on duty tonight?"

He smiled, walking over to her. "Yeah. Ever since Tom pulled the stunt he did, I've had to put in a LOT more hours. Let me tell you, he's got a LOT of people pissed right now." he went on. "But⋯. we're not here to talk about him. What's bugging you today?"

She took a deep breath, before answering him. "Basically, I feel like I'm pregnant. But I know I couldn't be."

"How long ago have you been sexually active?"

She shook her head. "It wouldn't matter, Steve. I'm 47...I'm too old to be pregnant."

"I've heard of crazier things," he went on, examining her sides, stomach and her heart. "I'll order a urine sample, and take some blood…just to be sure," he said, setting a hand in his jacket pocket. "So…have you heard anything—at all…from Tom?"

She closed her eyes, wishing everyone would stop asking her that.

"No. I haven't."

Dr. Romano looked down and gently patted her knee. "Ok. Hang tight dear. We'll get those tests ordered."

She took a deep breath, releasing it after he left…. reaching deep within herself to relax….

Meanwhile a code blue was being put out a floor above, as a flurry of nurses and staff moved about, onlookers staring as Mark's body was covered and taken out of the room.

A dark haired young man in his late twenties emerged, rushing down the corridor, only to slow down as he watched the scene with dismay.

"Dammit…I'm too late," he muttered to himself….

Greg had packed what little he'd come with, plus a few souvenirs of his first trip to LA, Elissa had gotten him. Then an hour later, the two were on their way to the airport.

"I feel like we've switched places," Greg jokingly said, as they drove.

Elissa smiled, knowing he was referring to when he had come to get her from the airport in St. Louis, just weeks ago. "Yeah, we have," she went on, coming to a stop. "It would have been nice, if you could have come with us though. Can you imagine the fun we would have had in the Virgin Islands?"

Greg had to laugh. "Yeah. All the while, the media could snap more pictures of us, leading to more speculation about my relationship to you, and Kevin could get insanely jealous."

She laughed. "Kevin's not jealous of you,"

Greg bit his lip, looking down and wanting to say, "He should be", but refraining. He had cared for Elissa for years as a sister⋯.then seeing her picture with Kevin in the gossip column of E News had done something to him. He knew then, how lucky of a man Kevin was.

"Greg?"

He turned to look up at Elissa, with her trademark smile that he knew deep inside made all the men go wild.

"We' re here⋯We' d better go in so you can catch your flight⋯."

Kevin worked for quite a while that afternoon, finally stopping to rub his eyes. He let out a breath, just as the phone rang again. He picked up, taking care of more business. He finally ended the call, and went to the bathroom, before grabbing a drink out of his mini bar.

They left early the next morning, so odds were he' d better get some sleep. It had been a long day and even longer night. He finished off his drink before undressing to his briefs and collapsing into bed.

After taking both tests Monica sat in her room and waited for nearly an hour before Dr. Romano came back with her results. He smiled.

"Well, you' re definitely not pregnant," he went on. "But⋯. something did come up in your lab work that I need to be concerned about."

She blinked, horror filling her eyes. "Oh God⋯. what is it?"

He hesitated, before going on. "There⋯. were traces of a very potent drug in your bloodstream. A drug that is rare, and only used in severe cases of nervous dementia. More than likely, this has been what's caused you to feel the way you have."

Monica looked at him, truly confused. "You're⋯.kidding⋯right?"

He shook his head. "No, I don't kid around with something like this," he went on. "Now Monica⋯You can be honest with me here⋯in fact, I need you to be. Have you been taking these drugs?"

Elissa walked with Greg to his gate where he was to board.

He sighed, turning to her. "You take care of yourself in the Virgin Islands ok?"

She smiled. "I think we'll do just fine. YOU take care too. You have a lot more on your shoulders than I do."

He hesitated, looking at the floor. "Yeah, I know. But I'll be all right. And so will your mom and Kayla too. I won't have it any other way."

She smiled, reaching out to give him a big hug and kiss on the cheek. She accidently left a reddish lip mark and had to giggle, trying to rub it out.

"What did you do?" Greg asked, suspiciously putting his hand up to it.

She shook her head. "I'm sorry. I'm just glad you don't have a girlfriend, or she'd be questioning you."

Greg smiled, shaking his head as his flight was called for the final time.

"I'd better get going. You take care sis."

She nodded. "I will…Bye."

She waved at him, watching until he disappeared down the long boarding gate area, before she turned back around to head back to the car.

Little did she know at the time, the next time she saw Greg….he'd be saving her life…

Kayla awoke late the next day, allowing herself more sleep. For the past several mornings she had been awaking early to go see Mark.

She sat up and stretched before going to the kitchen where Celia and her mom were, fixing brownies.

"Hey Kayla. Mom's making brownies for the youth picnic at church. You want to go?"

She nodded. "Sure. It sounds fun."

Celia showed her excitement, bouncing up and

down as her mother poured the batter into a brownie pan to bake. Kayla grabbed herself some juice, and right after she did this was when the call came in.

It was Celia' s mother' s friend that worked in the hospital. Her mother' s jaw dropped, as she stared at Kayla.

"Oh my God⋯. "

Meanwhile, at a hotel in town the same young guy who had rushed up to the scene in the hospital as they took Mark' s body out, came down into the lobby and picked up a copy of the paper. He leafed through it shakily until he found what he was looking for.

There was a short article about Mark, talking about his mysterious death. They were still investigating how he died.

He took a hand through his hair. He should have come before now. He should have done something the moment he saw that book come out on the market.

He set the paper down and left the lobby.

Elissa awoke the next morning yawning. Kevin

was already awake and had tossed a pillow at her playfully, yet firmly telling her to get up. After about an hour they were on the plane, heading towards the Virgin Islands.

Elissa sat, primping and checking her make up in her compact, as Kevin remained on his laptop···. still working. She finally set her compact down, and put her head on his shoulder looking over the screen.

"What are you working on?" she asked.

"I'm emailing my boss. Telling him, we're on our way, and giving him input on a few things he wanted."

She lightly smiled, gazing at his screen. She then turned to him, playing with his ear tracing her finger along it.

"You know, I've been thinking some about our wedding···. I think a Virgin Islands wdding would be perfect. I can fly my whole family in for it. It would be a blast."

Kevin clicked send on the email. "Yeah, it would be. But that nutso brother of yours won't be there."

At the mention of him, Elissa felt like she had a lump in her throat. She turned to face forward, and suddenly Kevin looked at her.

"I'm sorry baby···look, can we not even TALK about your family? I mean, this is like our vacation, you know? And besides···I really never planned to have ANY family at our wedding. We don't need them. Just a quiet ceremony, with you and me."

She just sat there, not saying a word⋯unable to believe anything he had just said. She then felt him squeezing her leg affectionately.

"Now come on⋯. let's have some fun and relax from here on out⋯We deserve it baby⋯"

Chapter 7

Monica stared back at Dr. Romano, horrified. "Steve…Of course not! I can't believe you would even consider such a thing!"

He let out a reluctant breath. "Monica…. it's no secret you've been through an enormous deal of stress lately. Even the least suspected person can turn to pretty desperate measures in desperate times."

She shook her head. "I can assure you…. I haven't been doing drugs. I've drank some, but never done drugs."

She got up, and started to dress.

"Monica…. I'm not accusing you here, I just want to help. I found traces of a potent drug in your system and as a doctor, I have to have some concern," he went on, hesitantly. "Besides…there's another factor here,"

She stopped, in only her bra and pants turning to look at him. "What?"

He bit his lip, a grim look in his eyes. "The drug I found in your system…is a match to one that has been short in our pharmeceutical inventory off and on for a long while…. up until Tom disappeared…"

Kayla stood there feeling floored, saddened, and partially relieved all at once. Celia and her mother gazed back at her.

"Are you ok hon? Do you want to talk to our pastor?"

She blinked and looked down. "I…. don't know."

Celia exchanged glances with her mother.

"Kayla…. I'm real sorry. I'll go with you if you want to talk to Pastor Cliff."

Kayla shook her head though.

"I…. don't have to talk to anyone." she said, slowly turning in a daze, to go back to Celia's room, leaving them to watch her helplessly…

Warm sunny breezes met Elissa and Kevin as they arrived at the airport in the southern part of The Virgin Islands. Kevin hailed them a taxi, that took them to their hotel.

Not even five minutes after they arrived, Kevin's cell phone was ringing. Kevin talked on the phone, laughing as they made their way up to their room which overlooked the amazing beach behind the hotel.

Kevin went into the bathroom···.still on the phone, emitting a slightly dissatisfied look from Elissa···.until he finally came out, telling the person they would see them soon.

She gazed at him, blinking in question. "I take it···.you have to go to a meeting?" she guessed, sitting down.

He smiled at her. "Nope···.Get yourself changed···We're going out to dinner with Kitus···"

Greg arrived back in St. Louis, with dread in the pit of his stomach. He drove past the Harner residence, still seeing yellow tape up. He released a shaky sigh, driving past what he knew was a news van. He didn't even look their way. He didn't want to talk to anyone. He just wanted to get to Monica, and make sure she was ok.

He then made the turn to head to St. Louis Memorial···

Not long after Greg drove down the street where the Harners had once lived in peace and harmony, another car approached slowly and pulled over to the curb. The same guy from the hospital and hotel got out and stared up at the house. It had taken him a while to find the address, considering they had an unlisted number. He'd had to go to the library and look up their name under the census.

He stood there, stock still, unable to believe he was actually there. He sighed, walking up to the house by the yellow tape, totally ignoring it, and hesitating as he stood by the door. It was obvious no one was there, hence the yellow police tape.

So why was HE still there and not leaving? He had to get in touch with the Harners somehow. He just didn't see any other way. He hung his head···

"Who is this?" John Keller, a reporter for channel four news in St. Louis took note of the mysterious dark haired guy standing in front of the Harner residence.

His assistant, who was munching away on a roast beef sandwich, looked out the window. "Probably just another one of these weirdo fans of Elissa's the police have had to drag off. I wouldn't think anything of it."

John continued to gaze at the stranger though, who was now hanging his head. He sat up more. "Nooo···. Something tells me this guy is different. I'm going to go talk to him."

Before his assistant could swallow the bite in his mouth he was chewing long enough to protest, John was climbing out of the news van, and heading towards the house⋯

Monica was walking out of the hospital as Greg drove up.

"Oh my God⋯.Greg!" She practically broke down in tears as she rushed forward to embrace him.

"Hey Monica⋯.What's going on? Has the doctor looked at you?"

She sniffed, and nodded.

"Let's just get out of here and go back to your place⋯I'll tell you everything there.."

Celia slowly opened the bedroom door to find her friend lying on the bed, her face away from her.

"Kayla?"

Getting no response from her friend, she went over to sit beside her.

"Kayla? Is there anything you want? Mom's got the brownies in the oven, and she promised you first dibs,"

Kayla slowly turned to look at Celia. "There was so much I had yet to talk to him about."

Celia just looked down. Kayla turned away again.

"I don't know what to think about anything anymore. My dad's missing, my half brother is dead, my other brother is in L.A. with Elissa, and my mom is all screwed up in her own way," she went on. "Last time I was there, she called me Elissa at one point. I said I was Kayla. She's losing her mind,"

Celia stared at her, not knowing what to say. Everything got silent after that, until a cell phone was heard ringing. It was Kayla's but she was making no move to answer it.

Celia then rose, going over to Kayla's purse to grab the phone and glance at the number popping up on it⋯..

Elissa let the other end of the phone ring until her sister's voicemail came on, and she left her a message. "Hi sis, it's Elissa. I just wanted to call and talk, see how you were. Um⋯I'm in The Virgin Islands right now with Kevin. He's on business, filming his first movie with Kriterion. So⋯I guess I'll try you later.

Love you. Bye."

She hung up and stared at the phone. She had went to dinner with Kevin and a few of the people from Kriterion···then they had dispersed into business leaving Elissa alone.

She hesitated, sitting there in the lounge of the hotel. She had thought about calling Greg, but decided against it. It would be getting late there now anyways.

The waitress came back over, asking if she wanted anything else. Elissa shook her head, actually starting to feel a little queasy.

"No thanks," she replied, getting up to head back to their room···

Greg got Monica back to his apartment, asking if she wanted a drink or anything. She shook her head, sitting down as he grabbed the last can of diet pepsi.

"I can see I need to go to the store," he said, as he popped the top and sat next to Monica. "Ok. Tell me what's going on Monica."

She kept her gaze down.

"According to Dr. Romano, and all the tests they ran on me, there are traces of a potent drug in my body."

Greg blinked in disbelief. "A···.drug? What

drug?"

"Some⋯⋯drug used for nerves and dementia. And that's not the best part⋯." she went on, turning to him. "It's the same drug that has been short at times in the hospital's pharmacy, Steve said. Up until Tom left."

Greg's eyebrows raised. "So⋯what are they saying? You and my dad are drug dealers, or addicts?"

"Oh⋯. I don't know Greg! This is such a horrible mess⋯I never have done drugs, and as for the shortage⋯I know Tom wasn't doing them either."

Greg looked away, his eyes deep in thought. "Damn⋯. Why didn't I ever think of that?" he said to himself.

Monica turned to him. "What?"

He looked at her. "I never thought to look through dad's office⋯. there could be some clue of where he took off to⋯. as much as I hate to admit and face this, dad could be involved in something illegal," he went on. "Is the house still off limits? I noticed yellow tape was still around it earlier."

She sniffed and shrugged. "I don't know Greg. But can't you worry about it later? I need someone."

He looked at the pleading expression in her eyes, and for the first time he honestly felt a burning hatred for his father. How could he abandon this woman, not to mention his whole family?

"Come here," he said, wrapping an arm around her, as she hugged him emotionally.

Chapter 8

He stood there in deep thought trying to figure out what to do when he heard the voice.

"Excuse me! I'm John Keller, from Channel Four News…. Did you know the Harners?"

He turned to see the tv reporter coming towards him. He sighed, rolling his eyes. He should have anticipated this. The media hounding their house. But unfortunately…this may be his only way to get to them.

"I'm trying to get a hold of them…. I have some very important information for them.."

"Ok…Good work planning today Mr. Lytle. Tomorrow we'll meet at our first location spot."

Kevin shook hands with the other two, before starting to head towards the elevator. Before he could touch the button to close the doors, a voice cried out to him.

"Wait!"

Kevin looked up and held the doors open as another slim man, with a ball cap and sunglasses quickly hurried on. He wore a short sleeved polo shirt, black shorts and sandals, and looked like a normal smiling vacationer.

"Thanks man."

"No problem." Kevin replied. "Which floor?"

"Third."

"Hmm.. Same floor me and my girlfriend's on."

The other guy beamed. "Vacationing?"

"Well…. I'm here on business, but I'm trying to make it a vacation for me and my girl."

"Aw, that's sweet. I'm here on business myself."

Kevin nodded, glancing at the floor light as they went up and breathing a sigh of relief as they reached their floor. Kevin was first off the elevator, telling the other guy to take care and enjoy his trip.

"I plan on it," he said, hanging back to watch which room Kevin went in before going on down the corridor….

After getting Monica calmed down, he fixed her some soup and got her to rest. Once she was asleep he sat there in the living room, deep in thought.

He had to figure out a way to get into the

house. Into his father's den. He knew somehow it had to hold an answer to these accusations⋯as well as where his father possibly was.

His thoughts were interrupted by the phone ringing. He got up, answering it.

"Hello?"

"Hi⋯Greg?"

He blinked. "Yes? Who is this?"

"This is Debra Miller, Celia's mother⋯I was actually calling to see how Monica was,"

He hesitated, making a face. "Not⋯too well right now. But I'm here now, and⋯..I'm going to look after her. How's Kayla?"

She took a deep breath, after pausing. "Not very well, I'm afraid. I feel so helpless, Greg. I want to help her through this, but I-" she trailed off.

"Do you think I need to come over?" he asked.

"Yes, I think you should since you're back in town." she went on. "I just don't know how to talk to her after her brother died⋯"

Elissa had already fallen asleep by the time Kevin got back there. He stripped and got into bed beside her, but not automatically going to sleep.

He had to figure out a way to broach the

contract to Elissa. But how? He knew, despite the fact she posed nude for Playboy she wouldn't bend so easily for him on this…. even though it cost his career.

He let out a breath as Elissa stirred.

"Kevin?"

"Yeah…. I'm here baby," he answered her as she rested an arm across him and he returned the sleepy gesture, holding her….

John couldn't hide his excitement. He knew there was a story with this guy, he wasn't like the other nutso fans.

"Really? What kind of information?"

The other guy seemed really hesitant. "To be honest, I'd rather tell them. I don't want this dragged through the media first. They deserve better with all they've been through. Can you put me in contact with them?"

John stared back at the guy. "You're kidding right? Who are you? From the newspaper? Or better yet, some entertainment magazine?"

"No, I'm not a reporter. In fact, up until a few days ago, I was a computer tech support person for Dot Net Enterprises." he went on.

"Let's just say…. there's been a bad case of mistaken identity. I simply want to get the truth to an already hurting family," he continued. "And if you play your cards right, and help me out I can give you exclusive first rights to the story…"

When Monica awoke, there were thin lines of light reflecting on the floor through the blinds. She blinked, looking around.

She was in Greg's bedroom. He was no doubt on the couch. She slowly arose, holding her head as she walked out to the living room. There was a plate of eggs, toast and sausage on the table with some juice…. and a note. She walked over and read it.

"Monica, I fixed some breakfast for you. I went to take care of a few things. Be back later this afternoon.

Greg"

She looked at the food. The sight of it made her sick. And that made her feel bad, because she knew Greg had gone through some trouble to fix it for her. He was such a sweet boy.. …. he reminded her of the way Tom once was.

She closed her eyes. Her husband. Still missing. The hospital now suspected him and possibly her of…. God only knew what. Something horrible involving drugs from what Steven insinuated the previous day.

She took a deep shaky breath, sitting down to slowly eat what she could of the breakfast Greg had left⋯

Celia's mother opened the door that morning, looking relieved to see Greg.

"Oh Greg⋯She hasn't even come out of bed this morning,"

He sighed, nodding as she let him in.

"Celia got up today to go with her dad. She even seemed really sad and guilty about leaving, but I told her you would be coming over. I don't think she would have gone if it weren't for that,"

He only smiled, wanly. "So⋯she's up in the bedroom?"

"Oh yeah⋯upstairs, the first door on the right."

He nodded again, thanking her as he headed up to see what he had to deal with⋯

Kevin awoke the next morning to find the bed beside him empty. He got up and went into the bathroom, hearing the shower going. He slipped in beside Elissa who gasped in surprise.

"Oh, you scared me! I thought you were still asleep."

"Surprise⋯Morning Beautiful," he said, enveloping her in a kiss.

She looked up at him. "How did yesterday go?"

He smiled. "Great. We meet on location today with some of the stars. We should be done though by late afternoon. Which⋯.gives us tonight to spend together," he said, stepping up closer to her in the shower, his hard erection moving up against her bare front.

She swallowed, looking down. "So⋯you'll be busy today?"

He gazed at her. "Well yeah. I do have to work here too, Elissa. We wouldn't even be here if it weren't for my job."

She kept her gaze down, turning to step out.

"You gonna be ok?" he asked her.

"Yeah, sure⋯" she said, and after a few more moments he heard the door shutting⋯

Kayla's eyes bolted open wide upon hearing her brother's voice through the closed door. She quickly leaped up, scrambling for the door.

"Greg! You're back!" she said, actually

glad to see him, wrapping her arms around him.

"Hey kiddo. I heard what happened."

She gazed up at him. "Did···. they tell you I was going to see him?"

He nodded. "Yeah."

She hung her head. "You're not mad?"

He shook his head. "No. I'm more worried about you."

Kayla made a wry face. "Things have been such a mess. Mom's going nuts, you and Elissa both left, dad took off···. I had no one else to talk to. Mark was all I had," she went on. "I felt like my whole family deserted me."

"Aw Kayla···. I didn't mean to make you feel that way. I just figured you coming here, meant you wanted to be with your friend."

She shrugged. "Part of me did. I feel like I lost touch with everyone. Celia was the only one there for me." she went on. "I already felt abandoned. Mom and everyone kept something that huge from me all my life. I think Mark would have talked more to me, but-"

Greg shook his head, putting an arm around her. "Don't worry about it. I'm back here, and I'm going to take care of you and your mom." he went on. "But···. I did want to find out something."

She gazed up at him with big questioning blue eyes. Nearly the same expression he had seen on her mother last night.

"What?"

He   sighed,   apprehensively.   "Is there⋯. anything you need to get back at the house?"

He watched and waited outside the corridor.

Twenty minutes after Elissa left the room, Kevin followed. As he disappeared down the hall, he quickly got up sliding through the door right before it closed.

He worked quickly, taking the small web camera out of his pocket and discreetly putting it behind a potted plant in the room. He stood back, trying to judge the angle he had set it at. It looked pretty damned accurate. At least accurate enough for what he had planned.

He had overheard Kevin talking to the other guys from Kriterion the previous day. He'd barely have time to take Elissa out, let alone kiss her while they were there⋯. which made his plan so much easier.

With a wicked, knowing smile he slunk right back   out   of   the   room⋯.

Chapter 9

Kevin made his way to their first location spot, the whole time his mind on Elissa. He fumed with himself. He hated not being able to be there for her on this trip···.but hell, she should have expected this.

He made up his mind to make reservations for them for dinner that evening. He had to get her in a better mood for what he had yet to bring up to her.

Elissa had changed into a two piece, with a flowery wrap around her waist, and flip flops as she went down to the pool. She sat down on one of the chaise lounges, smearing sun tan lotion over her arms, and legs before laying back with her shades on. She started to actually relax until she heard young giggling as her shades were removed.

She opened her eyes to see a little boy, no more than five or six, looking at her bashfully holding her shades. Before she could utter a word to him, a young woman hurried over, with an apologetic smile.

"I'm so sorry···Michael, give the girl her
glasses back!"

He looked up at his mom sadly.

"But I want them!"

Elissa had to laugh. That's when the woman
blinked in recognition.

"You're···..that one girl···. The one who was
just in that movie···"

Elissa sighed, realizing once again no matter
where she went, she'd run into someone who
recognized her through her stardom.

"Yes I am. Elissa Harner." She stretched
out a hand to shake the woman's. She smiled
shaking it then she frowned.

"Oh but···. you just had something bad happen
lately right? I remember reading about it in some
tabloid···Unfortunately I still read those things
even though they are mostly exaggerated stories."

Elissa gulped. "Yes···..Um···..My family
recently underwent an incident···. But now I'm on
vacation and···"

"Oh, of course, of course···. Sorry to even
bring it up. I don't suppose I···.. could have your
autograph could I?"

Elissa had nothing with her to autograph
anything. She used to carry something around with
her, but due to recent events and all···. she
hadn't done so. Then suddenly as if reading her
mind the woman pulled a pen and piece of paper out

of her bag she had slung over her shoulder.

"Who do I make it out to?" Elissa smiled and asked as she took the pen, poised to write⋯.

In the meantime, Kevin sat back drumming his fingers on the chair rest, watching as Tina Dunston one of the actresses in the new film read her lines doing a scene with Arnold Kraft, one of the main stars. Tina wasn't a horrible actress, but he had seen much better. She had done a short stint on a reality show, which had catapulted her to fame, much like many of present day actors and actresses coming into Hollywood.

Finally, the director called cut, breaking him of his thoughts as Clint Barston, one of the heads of Kriterion stepped up beside him.

"Amazing location Lytle. Your scout did a good job picking it."

Kevin turned to him. "Yeah, it works."

He remained quiet, and that scared Kevin.

"We need an answer on Elissa doing that scene, Kevin. Soon."

He bit his lip, looking down.

"I intend to ask her tonight."

He raised his eyebrows, eyeing Kevin skeptically. "You do realize if she doesn't do this⋯. it's your ass?"

Kevin felt himself turn red, answering him. "She will do it. Don't worry."

Clint just stuck out his chin defiantly as he turned to walk away, speaking to one of the assistants. Kevin released a breath, closing his eyes.

Why did he ever agree to this? Because he was desperate. The deal was too good to pass up. And he knew deep down, he hadn't gotten the deal because of his skill…. it was because of Elissa.

After speaking to the mysterious man, he left the premises and John Keller excitedly rushed back into the news van, where his partner sat dumbfounded.

"What the hell's going on?" his partner asked.

John didn't answer him. Instead he got on his cell phone dialing the number for his boss at the station.

"Yeah Phil…I just spoke to someone who's going to help me get a HUGE story on the Harners…I'm leaving the house now and heading back…"

In the meantime, the other guy walked off, wondering with a skipping beat of his heart if he was doing the right thing. He knew right now he had no other way to speak to the family. He didn't like going through the media either, but his options were very limited⋯now since the other one was dead.

He came to the corner, stopping to wait for the light to turn⋯. totally unaware to the fact that Greg and Kayla drove right past him⋯.

Greg listened to his sister heave a big sigh.

"Kayla⋯You ok? Are you sure you want to do this?"

She nodded. "Yeah. I've been wearing Celia's clothes and she's bigger than me. I know I look stupid," she said, looking down at the oversized wrestling shirt she wore, and the black baggy cotton shorts.

Greg smiled at her. "Nah, you look fine."

She smiled back at him as they pulled up in front of the house. Greg looked around and went "Hmmpphh," as Kayla turned to him questioningly.

"What?" she asked.

"Oh, I went by here earlier and there was a news van sitting here," he went on. "But it's gone. Which is good. Come on," he said, urging a reluctant Kayla out of the car···.

Elissa gave the young woman who introduced herself as Elizabeth Roman her autograph, and got her smudged up with fingerprints sunglasses back. She then went over to the bar, to try and clean them with some napkins. They were Gucci glasses, that cost her eighty bucks, so she wasn't about to ruin them. She cleaned them up the best she could, and returned to her seat.

She lied back down, and once again tried to relax and get the tan she had originally come out there for···

He walked out into the pool area and stood transfixed, staring at Elissa. A smiled touched the corners of his lips.

In just a matter of hours he would finally have it all. He couldn't wait, could barely contain his excitement. He wanted so badly now to just go over there, and introduce himself with the fake name he'd given the hotel when he made the reservations.

"Yeah hi. I met your boyfriend just the other day on the elevator. Real nice guy."

He bit his lip. He wanted to so bad. But he couldn' t. Not yet.

The time would come, he told himself. He just had to give it time….

Kayla slowly entered the house after Greg, looking around nervously. Everything was as it had been left, despite the yellow tape up outside. She looked at Greg who was already heading to their father' s den. He tried the door, unsuccessfully.

"Dammit! Locked…" he muttered.

"Are…. you sure we' re even allowed back in here Greg?"

Greg was still working with the door knob as he answered her. "Don' t be silly Kayla…this is our house. "

She looked at him worriedly, then averted her eyes.

"Kayla…why don' t you go on upstairs and grab your things? I have to figure out a way into dad' s office," he said.

She gazed at him unnervingly and with nervous concern, as she slowly made her way up the stairs….

John Keller made his way through the busy news room of Channel Four upon arriving, heading back to his boss's office. He knocked once before hearing in reply, "Come in!"

He walked in facing his boss, Phil Langford, the news editor in charge of approving any story for the Channel Four news. Phil was in his late fifties with already white hair, blue eyes and a reddish complexion. Word around the station was, he was an albino before his hair turned white.

He gave John a furtive look. "Ok. What have you got? And keep in mind, this had better be good, considering you left an assigned post."

He nodded excitedly. "Oh, it is.." he went on. "This guy walked up to the Harner house, and—there was just something different about him. He wasn't some crazy fan."

Phil shrugged. "So···.who the hell was he?"

John shook his head. "I still don't know. He won't give a name out."

"What?!"

John held his hands up. "Wait···.You haven't let me finish."

Phil shook his head, his already red face growing even redder. "You just left our post in front of the Harner house on the word of some guy who won't even give you his name, much less explain what big story he has to share?"

John sighed, then took out what the guy had

given him out of his back pocket, and handed it
over to his boss. His eyes grew so big he thought
they'd bulge right out of his head.

"Holy shit!", was all he could mutter….

Chapter 10

A half hour later Elissa gathered up her bag, and headed back to the room to change. Then she sat down, letting her eyes drift over to her phone. She reached over, punching in Greg's number.

"Hi, you've reached Greg Harner. You know what to do."

After the beep, and the rise in her heart she felt just hearing his voice, she spoke into the phone. "Hi Greg, it's me. I just wanted to call and see how things were with mom and Kayla⋯.and see if you've heard any word on dad. I⋯.miss you. Call me."

Her voice broke a little, before she hit the end button. She took a deep breath, closing her eyes⋯.totally unaware of the tiny web camera with it's red light, filming her the whole time⋯

Kevin stopped at the florist downstairs in the hotel first, buying a bouquet of red roses as he made his way towards the elevator. He rode up to their floor, then got off making his way towards the door.

Just as he was about to swipe his key card to open the door, the familiar voice from the other day spoke.

"Hey there…. Aw…. those for your girlfriend?"

Kevin turned to see the same man he'd held the elevator door open for the previous day. "Oh…. hey there. Yeah, I've been working all day and thought I'd take her out for a nice dinner by the beach."

"Ooohh…. yeah, that looks nice down there huh?" he went on. "I have an even better idea."

Kevin looked at him oddly. "Excuse me?"

He shook his head, holding up his hands. "Just…. hear me out, ok? I've already made reservations to eat at the Palisades Inn, just down the street. Unfortunately, my partner just called and told me he'd have to postpone…I hate for it to go to waste…please…you and your girlfriend go."

Kevin stood there, staring at him in shock. The Palisade Inn was one of the site locations for the movie he was working on. It was very elegant and pricey.

"Well…. Sure, I guess. You'll have to give me your name and room number, I'll pay-"

"No, no, you don't have to pay me back.

Thank you! I will call them now and tell them to expect you instead."

Before Kevin could utter another word, the guy took off. Kevin stood there trying to compose himself from the unexpected incident as he proceeded into the room···.

Greg growled under his breath, not able to get the door unlocked. He stepped away frustrated, and looked up towards the stairs where Kayla had gone. Then scratching his nose, he went back outside to the window in the den. He carefully started to raise the window. Luckily it went all the way up.

He propped himself up with all his strength, wiggling himself all the way through and ignoring the rip he felt on his jeans as he fell to the floor, knocking one of his father's expensive model ships he had made onto the floor, breaking. He swiftly got up and quietly started to sort through his father's desk area···.also ignoring the beeping of his cell phone in his pocket, signaling him of his voicemail.

He HAD to get to the bottom of things······. NOW···.

Kayla had slowly walked into her room, glad she didn't have to go any further down the hall near her parents room···.where it had happened. Mark had gone berzerk and shot himself. She squeezed her eyes tight, telling herself to go on, get what she needed and get back downstairs. Greg could be done and waiting for her by now. So she went with her instincts, quickly grabbing as much as she could in her pink and black backpack.

After filling it with as much as she could, she stepped out of the room, pausing by her mom's office···.the fan club for Elissa. The book still lied in there, on the chair near the desk. She walked in and picked it up, gazing at it before sticking it in her backpack as well.

She'd read the book fully now, herself. It was the least she could do for Mark, she decided as she quickly headed back downstairs···

Monica had laid back down for a little while to calm her unsettled stomach and nerves. She finally rose an hour later, and pulled on some sweatpants and a t-shirt of Greg's. She had to get out for some fresh air, she couldn't just stay there. She had to clear her mind, and she knew the perfect place to do it.

She grabbed her purse and left.

Elissa had been happily surprised by the flowers…and even more shocked when Kevin told her where they were going for dinner.

"The Palisades? Oh my gosh…I should change then. "

Kevin watched with a hungry smile as she changed into a short blue and white dress, and white sandals. Then he put out his arm to lead her out of the room.

"Allow me beautiful. " he said, with a flourish as he let her out the door first….

Meanwhile he sat on his bed in his room on his laptop smiling, as he watched them leave.

Yes! The plan was moving along perfectly! And as wierded out as Kevin acted, he hadn' t questioned it when he offered the reservations to him.

What he didn' t realize was, the reservations had been made for him and Elissa all along. With a smile, he shut his laptop, getting up to continue the next step of his plan…

Greg had looked through every unlocked drawer he could find, not running across anything but hospital files. He sighed, taking both his hands through his hair, deciding to take a break and see who had left him a message. It had been Elissa.

"Dammit!"

He quickly listened to the message, a small bit of worry coursing through him, hearing the emotional crack in her voice at the end. He slipped the phone back in his pocket. He couldn't deal with Elissa right now.

He couldn't deal with Elissa right now. He bit his lip, sitting at the desk and turning his father's computer on letting it boot up. After several seconds, the Windows symbol came on, and Greg leaned forward watching as all the icons popped up on the desktop. Everything appeared to be hospital files. Greg clicked on each one, going into them anyways.

It wasn't until he came across one file, named *M Record* that he finally hit pay dirt. He blinked, as an online journal….a medical record of….Monica came up. It was 57 pages long! But…. from what he was just scanning over, he knew something wasn't right.

"Greg?"

He heard Kayla's voice calling for him. He

bit his lip, quickly clicking print and reducing the size of the screen down so it wouldn't be shown as he got up to go let Kayla know where he was.

Meanwhile, he had ended up at the park not too far from the Harner residence. He sat down on a bench and gazed at the statue in front of him···..trying to figure out where everything went wrong.

Perhaps it was while he was too busy screwing around with Amanda···.the first one he had confessed everything to. Naturally, she had not given him much of a chance to explain, and freaked out over it.

He sighed heavily, leaning his head back. He had to keep telling himself this was the right things to do. It was hard though. He honestly didn't know how he was going to explain the truth to the Harners. But it had to be done.

He opened his eyes, bringing his head back up. He stood, prepared to go as he walked right into Monica, who stopped dead in her tracks upon seeing him. Her mouth dropped open in an 0 of wonder.

"Oh my God···" she said···recognizing him···..

Upon reaching the restaurant, Kevin and Elissa were promptly seated and brought a bottle of champagne.

"Here's to us." Kevin said, as they toasted their flutes.

Elissa sipped her champagne, then set the glass down.

"So···.how's the movie going?"

He smiled. "Wonderful···in fact, that's another reason why I asked you out tonight," he went on. "I may have a big part for you in it."

She gazed at him. "A···.part?"

"Yeah, a huge role. I mean, just think···.if you took this it would mean more time we could spend together. Just like the last movie, which I just heard today held it's first place steady at the box office for the fourth week in a row···.you're a hit baby."

She lightly smiled. "So···..What is this part? I was hoping this could be our vacation, you know? That we could talk a little more about our future. I wasn't exactly planning on working. I need a break Kevin, especially after what I've been through."

He nodded. "Baby I know, but I thought about it and I think this could be really good fo-"

She shook her head, holding up her hand.

"Woa, wait a minute Kevin. YOU thought about it? What about me? Did you even stop to consider I wasn't ready for another role yet?"

He sat there, staring her, then looked down. "Dammit Elissa···. You can't bury your freaking head in the sand, ok? So your brother's a damn nutcase and actually alive, and wrote a book to tell about it! Big deal! YOU are a beautiful, talented actress, you don't NEED that shit!!"

She blinked, gazing at him nastily. "Are you my boyfriend or my agent? No, wait···. I even think an AGENT wouldn't talk to me the way you just did!"

Kevin shook his head. "Look, I'm sorry baby···. I just don't want to see you shrivel up and not do anything anymore. This role is not that much, it's just one scene."

Elissa turned watery eyes away, glancing off in another direction.

"Come on Elissa···. Do it for me···. please?"

She kept her eyes averted. Kevin sat there waiting, then finally shook his head when she remained silent.

"Ok. Fine. Pack your damned bags."

She turned to face him sharply. "What?"

He stared at her through evil slitted glaring eyes. He was through begging, through being sweet to her. To hell with it.

"I said, pack your damned bags Elissa···. I am

not out of a fucking job, thanks to you and your
stubborn   paranoia!"

Chapter 11

Greg drove Kayla back over to Celia's···.to find no one home.

"Do you have a key?" he asked.

"No, but there's supposed to be a key rock out here. Celia's mom showed it to me one day."

Greg sat there, anxious to get the papers somewhere to read···.then call Elissa back. "Well, I can stay here long enough to make sure you get in. If you need anything else, you know my number."

Nodding silently, she got out of the car and headed up to the front porch. He watched as she knelt down, picking up something and retrieving a key from it. She waved at him as she unlocked the door and stepped inside.

Greg smiled, holding up a hand to wave back, then pulled away from the curb···.

Kevin got up and stormed away from the table before he made much more of a scene. He was fuming though, deep down. He had helped Elissa become what she was right now, and she couldn't return the favor.

He was so mad it didn't even bother him that he had left Elissa to pay for their dinner. In fact, this little unintended gesture made him feel a little better.

He kept walking 'til he found himself at the bar down the street from the Inn. He didn't pause for long outside the place before going in……

Monica's shocked expression turned to one of a widening smile.

"Peter Woodland…. My God, is it really you?"

He smiled at her. "You actually remember me?" he asked.

"How could I forget you? I used to babysit you, and you were Mark's best fri-" She cut herself off, remembering everything and hanging her head quickly. "Anyways…yes I remember you. I always loved you like a second son."

He kept smiling. "How have you been? I mean…. I heard about what happened…. I can't say it's not a big reason for me even coming back here,"

She bit down on her lower lip, sinking onto a bench. He sat beside her.

"The last few weeks…. . have been a

nightmare," she went on, staring into space as if reviewing a horrid memory from years past, or maybe even recent.

"I'm sorry Mrs. Harner···. About everything."

She turned to face him. "You're what now···..30?"

"Thirty one actually···. Remember? My birthday fell a few days before Elissa was born."

Her eyes lit up. "Oh yes···I should have remembered that! We had to move your party because I was supposed to have Elissa that day, and my water broke while I was planning your Transformer party···" She laughed at the memory. "Anyways···. I think you're old enough to call me Monica now."

He nodded, smiling. "Ok Monica···. You up for some coffee?" he asked. "My treat···"

Meanwhile, down at the morgue the coroner was looking over paperwork pertaining to Mark's body. He had been behind all week, and was anxious to get this done. Unfortunately he was running across more of a problem though.

Picking up the phone he dialed the number for the lab. On the third ring a female's voice answered.

"This is Rob, down in the morgue. We have a

problem here…"

After he relayed the situation over to her, she told him to hold on. He waited a few minutes before another voice, this time male came on the line.

"Hey Rob…. Sorry about the delay. Um…As for the problem on the body you are referring to, there's a reason for it."

Rob shook his head, in question. Body he was referring to?

"Look…I've been behind all week, I just want to get this handled and done. What's up Dan?"

There was a long pause before Dan from the lab replied. A pause so long Rob just knew they had fucked something up and this couldn't be good.

"That body…. is NOT Mark Brewster's…."

After paying the waiter, Elissa went into the bathroom where she slammed the door shut and started sobbing.

She knew this trip was a bad idea. She just knew it!

She sat on the toilet seat wiping her mascara smeared eyes. Fucking great! Now she'd look like a damn raccoon if she went out of there! If some other vacationer had a camera on them, they could snap her picture and make a fortune with the tabloids.

Elissa sighed shakily, hearing a few women come in. She couldn't stay in there forever. With a deep breath she got up, putting on her sunglasses and walking out of there···.

Greg pulled into a rest stop, where he got out to use the bathroom and check out the rip in his pants. It was on his right back side, showing his black briefs. Thankfully Kayla hadn't noticed it.

There was a coffee machine there at the rest stop, which he took advantage of. Inserting change for a cappucino, he grabbed the cup after it was prepared automatically and carried it back to his car, where he debated whether to start reading the medical record on Monica or call Elissa back. He was worried about Elissa, but knew he couldn't be out long either and needed to check on Monica as soon as possible. And he wasn't about to read this around her. She had a right to it, but something told him not to have it around her right now.

So, logic winning over Elissa, he picked up the papers from the backseat, settling back to read then…

"I can't get over how much this city has changed over the years…You actually have a Starbucks here," Peter said, sitting down across from Monica in the well known restaurant.

Monica smiled. "Yeah. Elissa got addicted before she left for Hollywood….and I have to admit, so did I." she chuckled.

Peter smiled, sipping his iced latte.

"So, Pete….How is your family all doing?"

He looked down. He knew this would come ultimately. "My dad died soon after we moved away….truck accident," he went on. "My mom passed away a little over a year ago. Cancer."

Monica's mouth dropped open. "Oh my God Pete….I had no idea…"

He shrugged. "It's not like we kept in contact."

Monica blinked, and looked away. "Your mom tried to call me several times last year…I never got back to her. I was so busy running Elissa's fan club, and trying to keep my decorating business up..Oh my God, she was probably calling to say good bye!"

Monica couldn't hold back a sob. Peter blinked, averting his eyes.

"It's ok Monica. How could you have known?"

She sniffed, grabbing a napkin and wiping her eyes. "I know, but still···That must have been so hard on you,"

He kept his gaze down. "Yeah. It's definetly not been easy···"

It then remained silent between them for several moments, until Monica broke the silence. "Ok···. So, what have you been doing with your life? Have a girfriend? Job?"

He looked at her. "I did."

She gazed at him in question. "Did? What happened?"

He took a deep breath. He was not ready to go into this. At least not there.

"It's···..a really long story Monica. Can we head back to your place and talk?"

Kevin was on his third or fourth drink···he wasn't sure which, he was starting to lose count···when he heard her voice.

"I didn't expect to see you here."

Kevin turned to see, none other than one of the stars of the film he was producing, Tina Dunston. She stood there, eyeing him with a sexy smile. Kevin was pretty sure it was that smile and her looks that got her the part in the movie.

He smiled right back at her. "Well….can' t say I expected to see you either,"

She smiled, sitting beside him at the bar. "Two Smirnoffs please," she signaled the bartender. "You like Smirnoffs right?"

Kevin nodded, as the bartender slid two bottles over to them.

"So….where' s your girlfriend?"

Kevin' s face darkened. "What girlfriend?"

She shook her head, as if it was self explanatory….which it was, but he was drunk. "Elissa? You know, the blonde you came with that' s supposed to be in our movie?"

He shook his head. "There is no girlfriend. We' re through."

Her eyes widened. "Really? I….guess that WOULD explain why you' re here," she went on, sitting up more and sticking her breasts in his face closer. "Well….Sorry to hear that. But….maybe you two just weren' t meant to be. Maybe someone else is meant to be with you."

Kevin smiled. "You think?"

She leaned over more closely to him. "I feel pretty confident. In fact, something tells me if we leave now, and head back to my room, there' s a good chance your sexy ass will get laid."

Kevin smiled at her, the Smirnoff, and tonic he had been drinking before she showed up clouding his head…..Clouding everything but his hormones.

"That's the best idea I've heard yet during this trip," he said, nearly falling off the stool to follow her out of the bar…

With the tint of her sunglasses, it was already hard to see inside the place to leave. And she was getting that queasy feeling again that she had gotten the day they arrived. She thought it was anxiety, but now she was starting to question it.

She had to stop and brace herself against what she thought was a building's wall…but it felt too soft, like…a human's chest. She jumped and started to say "Excuse me," and apologize, but before she could say anything she felt something soft and weird smelling hit her nostrils…. then she totally blacked out….

After sitting there for nearly an hour at the rest stop, Greg read all the pages of the medical journal. He sat there, in shock.

"My God," he said, taking a hand through his hair.

The journal was a record of Monica's history

since she had become his father's patient, clear up to just under a year ago. She had been treated for various mental conditions and symptoms not even his own father had told him about. Greg figured not everything was his business⋯.but still, it left Greg suspicious.

Monica had been on several different medications after claiming not to be. He had to get back into the house⋯.and he needed to get back to his place, and talk to Monica⋯..somehow bring this up in a way to not alarm her—if that was even possible.

He started the car, and headed out of the rest stop⋯totally forgetting to return Elissa's call⋯⋯

Chapter 12

Celia's mother had left Kayla a note, saying there was chicken casserole in the microwave for her to heat up. They would all be gone for an unknown amount of time, due to Celia's grandfather having a heart attack. He was in a hospital in Kansas City.

She wasn't very hungry at the moment so she just grabbed some Mountain Dew out of the fridge, going into Celia's room. She set the soda on Celia's nightstand, and retrieved the book out of her bag.

She stood still, just staring at the bound edition in her hands. Slowly sinking down onto the bed, she opened it and began to read⋯.

He couldn't get over how easy this was. Fate was working right for him for a change.

He had to carry Elissa back through the hotel. With her sunglasses on, no one could tell it was actually her. He did have to stop and try to overcome one more hurdle though before his plan could really begin. Luckily it went through as well.

"Mr. Lytle is busy in a meeting with the crew of his film⋯.Elissa had a spell on the set, and he asked me to discreetly get her back to her room,"

The woman at the desk started to jump, but stopped.

"Who are you?"

He smiled, remembering his response to the desk clerk as he now lied Elissa right where he wanted her, adjusting the web camera. She had promptly let him in, after he had told her who he was. And he knew Kevin's stupid ass wouldn't be back for a while, not after what he paid Tina to keep him busy⋯.no matter what.

He finished adjusting the web camera, and turned to stare at Elissa, her sunglasses still hiding her smeared eyes.

"The truth's finally going to come out, my dear Elissa⋯.all we're waiting on now is you, the star⋯.to wake up⋯"

Monica wasn't sure how Greg would react to her bringing Peter over there, and told him she was staying with someone. "My place has been roped off as a crime scene," she admitted.

He nodded solemnly. "Yeah, I know. I was

over there earlier." he confessed, now starting to feel really bad about what he'd done. Of course, he didn't expect to run into Monica this easily! Let alone, her actually remember him.

"Really? You were?" she went on. "How···.did it look?"

He shrugged. "Fine, except for the grass maybe needing mown. You would have never known it was the place of a crime scene···minus the yellow tape."

She looked down. Then an uncomfortable silence fell between them.

"Monica···.why don't you come back to the hotel with me? It's quiet, and I can get us room service, and we can talk."

She looked at him, debating his offer. "Ok," she finally said, as he led her out of the park···.

In the meantime, at the news room in St. Louis Phil sat at his desk, over his tenth cup of coffee, boring a hole staring at what John Keller had brought him earlier that day. He was debating whether to put it on the air, but it would raise too many questions as to how they came across it. As desperate as he was for a good news story, he wasn't unethical.

With a frustrated growl he sat back, a hand to his chin. Who WAS this guy? Whoever he was, why did he need to go through them to contact the Harners, when it was obvious he had connections to them somehow?

Unless···.they got severed somehow. What he gave John was proof positive he had known the Harners at one time, or at least Elissa. He chewed on his lip, glancing at the time as he left the small box containing the locket on his desk. He went out the door, locking up···.

Not wanting to chance going by the house again, Greg headed back to his apartment. Leaving the records in the car for the time being, he went up to his place to find Monica gone. He put a hand to his head, a little frantic.

"Don't totally bug out···.she probably needed some fresh air, and went out for a walk," he tried telling himself as he sat down. Figuring this would be a perfect time to return Elissa's phone call, he grabbed his phone and dialed in her number···.

Meanwhile, as he was busy on his laptop

getting everything set up, he stopped for a second, hearing the tiny tune of a cell phone. He jumped up, racing over to the bed where Elissa's purse was, dumping it's contents out as her tiny pink phone fell out. He sighed, holding it in midair.

This was one thing he had never considered in all of this. He opened the phone to see Greg's number lit up. With a grim look, he closed it and threw it over in the corner. He'd destroy the phone later, if it came down to it. He wasn't going to let ANYTHING stand in his way….

Kayla had gotten through the first three chapters of the book before she got hungry. Even then, she took the book with her to the kitchen to warm up the casserole.

She sat at the table, reading it as she slowly ate. She thought it was an incredible story so far. Mark had been a very talented writer. Because it was fiction, and the fact she wasn't around throughout the course of events it was based on, it didn't seem to bother her nearly as much as it probably should have, reading it.

She was nearly through the fourth chapter when Celia's mother called to see how she was, and tell her they wouldn't be back for a few days.

"How is he?" Kayla asked.

"Not very well I'm afraid⋯. The Doctor thinks this is it." she went on. "He's had a bad heart for years, so I expected this day to come at some point." she continued. "Are you sure you're going to be ok sweetie?"

"Yeah, I'm fine. My brother got me a few extra things. I'm just glad you're letting me stay."

"You're more than welcome sugar. Besides, now we'll need someone there to house sit. Can you get the mail, and feed the fish and Roxy?"

Roxy was their little Chihuahua.

"Sure."

"Great. Thank you. I'll give you a call with another update in a few days."

They hung up and Kayla returned to the book. She had a few days to finish reading it.

Perfect⋯.

Finally satisfied with the angle and website he'd created, he turned back to Elissa. He walked over, and carefully removed her sunglasses. He tried hard not to laugh at the smudges of mascara lining her face. He had to do something about that. He went into the bathroom, and grabbed a rag, wetting it with some soap as he took it back out to wash her face.

"Uhhhuuuhh…" She started to moan, and stir as he did this, but he continued to try and clean off her face as much as he could.

"Umm…. Uhhhh…"

She started to open her eyes, blinking as some soap apparently got in them, tearing them up. He quickly took out his handkerchief and wiped them too.

Elissa lied there now, slowly blinking. "What happened? Kevin?"

He shook his head. "No. Kevin's not here."

She slowly turned to face him, and her face registered startled recognition as her eyes fell on him.

"Dad!"

Monica followed Peter into his hotel room.

"Wow…. You certainly got a lavish room," she said, taking in the surroundings. It consisted of a huge queen sized bed with a dark green bedspread, a TV in the wall across the room, as well as a small mini bar.

"Want a drink?" he offered, thinking for what they were about to discuss, she would need it. But she shook her head.

"No, I shouldn't. Next thing you know, I'll be getting accused of being an alcoholic,"

Peter shook his head, then told her to have a seat. He sat in an armchair across from her in the corner.

"Monica···.what I have to tell you···..goes back years. When Mark and I were babies."

She sat, gazing at him and listening intently. He hesitated, going on.

"My dad was an agent with the FBI. We were sent to live there next to you, your husband and Mark." he went on. "He used me to spy on you guys, to befriend Mark and get information."

Monica's brows wrinkled in confusion, as she gazed back at him questioningly. "What? Why?"

He bit on his lip. "It was all a huge mistake Monica," he went on, emotionally. "We had the wrong man···."

Greg sat there, after dialing Elissa's number, blankly. Someone had picked up, then hung up. By the time he'd said hello, he got a dial tone in his ear.

Something wasn't right. He tried the number again. This time he got voicemail. Elissa's cheery voice told him to leave a message, and thanked him in advance.

"Hey sis, it's me. I⋯..hope everything's ok. I sensed it wasn't in your voice from your message. Please call me back whenever you get this. Love ya."

He hung up, feeling only mildly better. Perhaps her phone was messing up. It wasn't entirely impossible, considering she was clear out in The Virgin Islands, and Greg was on the fourth floor of a six story building. There could very easily be a connection problem. That's what he continiously told himself anyway, as he grabbed a sandwich to decide his next move.

Chapter 13

He smiled upon hearing those letters, forming that one word. "Hi Elissa."

She lied there still stunned, her head shaking. "What happened? You've had us all worried sick about you."

He sat there, gazing at her with a smile. He gently stroked the side of her face. "I'm sorry sweetheart. I hated to leave you in the midst of all that happened, but I had no choice." he continued, after some hesitation. "I assume you and your mother know the truth,"

She stared at him bewildered. "The truth?"

He eyed her. "That D.S. Kirk was really Mark. Your brother."

She blinked, then looked down. "I'm sorry to have to bring it up but⋯"

"You *knew* he was Mark?" she asked, now looking at him with fire in her eyes.

Her father gazed back at her. "Not at first Elissa⋯..not until I went to meet with him and talk to him more. It was little gestures he made that clued me into it. Plus, not to mention the book he wrote of course⋯..then I couldn't have come home and told you guys who he really was! It would have made matters worse. I kept it from you to protect you and your mother, and Kayla."

She stared at him, now confused. "And…that's why you took off?"

He sighed, closing his eyes. "No, my dear. Not entirely why at least…." he went on, looking at her. "I left, because your mother was dealing in drugs, and she's become addicted as well. I tried to stay and help her, but I found out she's been using my key card access to take drugs from the hospital. She has no idea what she's doing, and the hospital administrators would never believe me and even if they did, I'd be fired," he went on, hoping the web mic was capturing his voice well enough. "So sweetie, I had no choice but to leave. I just hope you can find it in your heart to forgive me…."

John Keller was standing in the shower that evening, pretty satisfied with himself. This would put him on the map, nabbing the story of Elissa Harner. It was already rumored "Secrets Unearthed" was based off of Elissa's past. Most rumors turned out to be true eventually, especially in Hollywood. This wasn't Hollywood, but Elissa was a hot actress right now. She was from St. Louis as well.

He shut off the water nozzle stepping out, when he heard his girlfriend's voice calling out for him. Putting a towel around his waist, he rushed out to find her on her laptop, on the bed. She motioned for him to hurry over beside her, which he did.

"What–" he started, but stopped once he saw the screen.

It was Elissa's official website···. with a live web cam···.

Greg decided to hang around an hour longer to see if Monica showed back up. At five minutes til the top of the hour, he started to get worried. Where could she be?

"Maybe she went shopping or something and lost track of time." he tried telling himself, releasing a breath. It still worried him though, after all that happened, and especially after what he read in the report. He doubted the police would do anything about it, considering she hadn't been gone 24 hours.

Greg picked up his keys and left, knowing what to do···

Monica sat there, tears glistening her eyes as she gazed back at Peter. "What?" was all she barely managed to whisper out.

He closed his eyes, raking a hand through his hair. He took a deep breath before beginning the long story. "You know that···.Seth was gambling. Well···.there were reports of a guy with Seth's description who had broken into a few homes, taking money, drugs, and other top secrets stuff. One of these homes belonged to my dad's boss, Frank Ellerson."

Monica looked at him in total bewilderment.

"Anyways···..me and my parents were living in St. Paul at the time, where I was born. Frank was my godfather so of course he was there for my birth."

Monica's eyes grew with recognition. "That's where Mark was born."

Peter nodded. "Yes, I know. And that day, Frank saw Seth. He tried to nab him outside the hospital but Seth got away, telling him he was mistaking him for someone else."

Monica now looked stunned and thoughtful. She had a very brief flashback of being in the hospital after giving birth, and Seth coming in to see her···.but he wasn't acting like himself. He had attributed it to being tired.

"So···.not long after I had been born···..I

don't think I was much older than about five or six months…. we were assigned to live next to you guys. Frank seemed adamant Seth was the man we were looking for, and once I saw that he gambled, I figured Frank had to be right."

Monica nodded. "Yeah…you know you're bringing back some long lost memories," she went on. "I was trying to get my business started up, and hardly paid much attention back then, and I also had to take care of Mark…. Seth had a lot of late nights, and half the time when we were together…. it was weird. But it was fun. It was almost like I was with two different people. But I always assumed it was Seth's mood, and of course Mark got that from him,"

Peter bit his lip, his gaze falling downward, with that same expression before he told her they had the wrong man.

"What Peter?"

He took a deep breath, looking up. "You felt like you were with two different people because…. you were…. "

Elissa sat up more on the bed. "What? Mom's a druggie?"

He nodded. "Yes hon. I'm sorry to have to be the bearer of bad news to tell you, but it's true. I didn't believe it at first either, then-I noticed the logs. All the times drugs had turned up missing and I knew I hadn't been in there as much as it said. Then I came home to find the drugs hidden in your mom's bureau. That's when I knew."

Elissa shook her head, getting up. "I can't believe this. I have to call Greg!"

Her father took her gently by the arm, stopping her. "No Elissa. Not now." he went on. "Please sit down, and hear what else I need to explain to you first…"

Kayla got to chapter 11, before her eyes started growing heavy, and she needed to use the bathroom. She went into the restroom and noticed the time. She decided to get ready for bed. Changing into her PJ's she crawled under the covers with the book to continue reading. A half hour later she had falled asleep, the book still in her hands….

Greg had made a few rounds, driving in his Sentra. It was starting to get dark, as he came upon the house again.

Yellow tape still stretched across it. He pulled over and shut off the car.

For some reason now, he felt better going into the house alone. He walked in, using his key and silently closing and locking the door behind him.

He had left the door to his father's den unlocked. He went inside, shutting the door behind him and rubbing his hands together as he headed back over to his father's desk. He re-looked through the drawers, just to ensure he hadn't missed anything. That's when the phone rang, startling him. Not the house's main line···.his father's private one in the den.

Greg sat there, still as a rock as his father's voicemail kicked on. *"Hi, you've reached the home office of Dr. Tom Harner. Please leave a message at the tone. If this is an emergency contact me on my cell at 555-2780."* After a long beep, a familiar voice that he couldn't place, spoke.

"Tom, this is getting out of hand. I can only hold off for you for so long, and cover. People are getting suspicious. Your cell phone is out of the area and I've called your office six times now···.either get back with me by tomorrow, or I'm sorry···I'm going to have to tell everyone the truth···."

"Oh my God···What is that?" John asked, staring at the screen over his girlfriend's shoulder.

"It looks like Elissa Harner, although I don't know what's up with her face···.as for the guy, I have no idea."

He shook his head, peering even closer and watching them. He had grabbed Elissa by the arm now, and that made John's heart thump.

"Wait···.Something isn't right here. Do you have better sound on this thing? Can you turn it up?"

She clicked on something, bringing the volume up.

"What are you talking about dad? Mom needs help, and the only one that can help her right now is Greg!"

"That answers who the guy is, but who's-"

"SShhh!!!" John hushed his girlfriend as he leaned in more to listen to the video stream···.

Peter got up, starting to pace. "Monica···.Seth Brewster was a non-identical twin to Elliot Stanton. They were separated at birth, both adopted. Of course, this information didn't come along until much later. Anyways····.when Elliot discovered he had a twin brother, he made use of the factor. He made the proper adjustments to his appearance, to the point no one could tell them apart. While you were pregnant with Elissa, this was discovered when my father was talking to Seth when he dropped by to pick Mark up one day····.we both overheard them talking about a previous discussion they'd had····..that Seth didn't remember at all."

Monica sat there, her eyes wide. "So····.you think they····.traded places?"

Peter set his jaw thoughtfully, biting his lip. "Not so much traded places, as Elliot snuck in when Seth was out gambling. It would explain what you said about the mood change,"

Monica put a hand up to her head, as if she was getting a headache. "Which means···Oh my God····.Could Seth still be alive?"

Peter sucked on his lips. "We···checked into that right after it happened. Unfortunately it was Seth who was killed."

Monica sat back then, looking deflated. "Oh my God····.And-you said it was while I was pregnant for Elissa, that you first noticed a difference in Seth?"

He solemnly nodded.

"And···this was-Oh Lord···"

Peter looked at her, as her face went two

shades whiter.

"Monica?"

She gripped the sides of the chair she was in so hard, her knuckles turned white. "The first night I noticed···. this difference with Seth, it was so subtle, like···. he was really wild. Seth was normally to himself and so sweet and gentle···. He was still that but···he was doing things he'd never done before, like···. he performed oral sex on me for the first time, which wasn't like him···. but I was in Heaven···"

Peter looked down. Suddenly, she seemed embarrassed.

"Anyways···it wasn't long after that night, I discovered···I was pregnant with Elissa.."

Peter looked up at her. "Seth never told you he was adopted?"

She shook her head. "No···His parents were dead, and that's all he'd ever tell me."

Peter sat down again. "And···you never had any paternity tests run for Elissa···"

"Because I had no reason to! I thought···. I was only involved with one man!"

Peter looked away as she suddenly got up.

"I···. have to get a hold of Greg···"

"Wait Monica," Peter said, stopping her in her tracks. He hesitated, getting up to face her. "There's···..a whole lot more to the story than even that," he continued. "I think you'd better sit back down⋯"

Elissa gasped as he threw her onto the bed, grasping her arms and tying them together, straddling her. "Dad! What the hell are you do–"

She was stopped by him clamping a hand over her mouth. "I don't want you calling Greg or anybody about this. I'm going to tell you what I want to do, ok? You going to trust me? Trust your father?"

She nodded as he finally let go of her mouth. "That's better," he said getting up and laying beside her. She lied there, still and quiet, just staring at him with tears running down her face. He leaned over, wiping her tears with his hand. "Darling, there's no need to cry. Just listen to me, please⋯." he went on. "What's happened has been⋯. so beyond my control. I guess I should just start out at the beginning. I mean, hell⋯.. I already know my job is history," he went on. "My real name is not Tom Harner. It's Elliot Stanton. I picked the name Tom Harner from an exercise in an old medical book. He was a fictional doctor in an example," he continued. "The man you know normally as your biological father was my twin brother Seth."

Elissa stared at him like he was crazy.

"What? Twin brother? You look nothing like the pictures of him."

He smiled. "That' s because we' re non-identical. I changed my features a little bit so your mom would still think I was Seth. I kept an eye on him while he went and gambled his stupid life away. Then, I' d keep your mom company." he went on with a sly smile. "Boy, did I keep her company. I didn' t realize she dabbed in drinking a little⋯" he went on. "Anyways, I discovered Seth was my twin brother purely by accident. We ran into-well, I saw him at the hospital apparently after you mother had Mark. Basically it helped me out some too. Whenever I needed a place to hide for a while, I' d take Seth' s place."

Elissa continued to stare at him, wide eyed. "But⋯. you⋯. don' t look anything like him⋯. I thought even non-identical twins had some resemblance."

He smiled again. "As a member of the medical community, you' d be amazed at the favors you can have done with plastic surgeons," He pulled a picture out of his wallet and showed it to her. "This is me with my first wife."

She glanced at the photo. He did look somewhat like Seth in that photo⋯. but there was another factor that bugged her. "That woman⋯. she⋯."

"⋯Is Greg' s mother⋯. yes." he replied.

"And…that's an entire other can of worms we need to go over…. but at some other point," he went on, getting up. "Truth be told Elissa, I need you and you need me right now. Kevin's gone, my medical career is over."

She shook her head. "I need you? I don't get this…you basically just told me you have lied to my family all these years, that technically you're my uncle, not my stepfather an—"

"Elissa, I AM your father!" he bellowed all of a sudden. "I had it checked and double checked through blood samples at the hospital, in secret! You and Kayla are my biological daughters…"

Chapter 14

The caller of the message just left on Tom' s machine still had their hand on the phone after hanging it up. The person got up and walked over to a framed photo on the wall, one showing Dr. Romano with a dark haired woman and two boys.

The person sighed. They were so foolish to *ever* agree to this. Sure, Tom had something on him if he let everything explode. They both had a lot to lose if he "squealed" on him, as Tom had put it, when he caught him late one night, taking some of the drugs.

The person hesitated in the semi darkened room, running a hand along the picture when a female voice called out for them.

"Steve? I' m home…"

John continued to watch the video feed in total awe. It was breaking up some, and that' s when he heard thunder outside. John strained to hear the next words come through when the power went out.

"Shit···.Where's my cell phone?" he sprang up, nearly stubbing his toe on one of his girlfriend's shoes as he searched through the darkness for his cell.

"John, what are you doing?"

"I'm calling my boss! He needs to know what we just saw!"

Finally he found the small phone, and picked it up, quickly dialing his boss's home phone.

"Fuck!" he cried out. "Power must be out all over St Louis···Damn, what a time for this to happen···.Did you see that?"

His girlfriend just sat there silent. He paced the room as his sight adjusted to the pitch blackness. Light illuminated the room every few seconds as lightning struck.

"" It was probably a publicity stunt, John."

He stopped, and shook his head. "No···. I don't think so."

"Why not? The whole thing could have been staged. She IS an actress you know."

John looked down. Could she be right? If that was the case, that guy at the Harner place···he could be part of it. And if he was, John fell hook, line and sinker. He took a deep breath. He couldn't even think that way right now.

He just shook his head, saying "Let's just go to bed baby···. I'm exhausted···"

A loud clap of thunder is what awoke Kayla.
She dropped the book to the floor, looking up. The
room was totally dark, besides the flashes of
lightning from outside illuminating the posters on
Celia' s wall.

Kayla slowly got up, and picked the book back
up. She lit a few of the candles in her friend' s
room, getting a little light once she realized the
power was out. She lied back down with the book,
and picked up right where she left off, only
glancing up once more as another loud clap of
thunder hit⋯.

Greg was preparing to call the number back,
when the power went out. Then he tried on his own
cell phone, only to get no signal. "Shit," he
muttered, getting up. There were flashlights in
the closet hallway. He just hesitated going there,
because it was still considered close to a crime
scene. There had to something else nearer.

He went through the lower floor of the house,
looking. He ended up in the kitchen. He stopped,
still seeing traces of dishes in the sink from
that last dinner with "D. S. Kirk". He went

through towards the laundry room, where he did manage to find a small flashlight. He picked it up, testing it and went back to his father's den.

He sat down at the desk. He now knew for sure his dad was hiding something. That call, the message had been proof. But of what? He sat there, shakily trying to think. He knew that voice. Who was it?

"Dammit," he muttered, taking his hands through his hair. The rain was pelting outside. He had to think.

He took the flashlight, and then started looking through his dad's bookcases. He'd looked everywhere else, not finding anything. As he came to the end of one shelf he found it. A 5 by 7 yellow envelope, wedged against the metal bookend. It had been there for quite some time because it took Greg some work getting it out, and when he did, part of it stuck to the metal shelf, tearing the envelope a little···.but not to the point Greg couldn't tell who it was from···.the very P.I. whom he had hired to look for Tom!

Elissa stared at him, nearly in disgust. She seemed speechless now, and he knew he had come to the point he needed to.

"Now Elissa honey···.. I know this may come as

a shock to you⋯. I mean, I know all those years, you called me daddy⋯. and for years I really wished that were true. You became so beautiful, you grew up to be so talented and successful. I envied my brother for being your biological father."

"Then one day⋯. My wife dropped a bomb on me. My wife of nearly eleven years," he continued. "She told me she was leaving me for another man⋯Greg's real father."

Elissa's facial expression changed upon hearing these words, as he went on.

"So⋯I had been seeing your mother anyways at this time, so it was no big deal that she was leaving me⋯.. but⋯." he continued after a pause. "It killed me learning Greg was not my real son. So after years of indecisiveness, I finally decided to have it tested. See if I was your real father. Every test came back with the same answer. Yes."

Elissa just stared at him, still speechless. He smiled to himself.

"I could never tell Greg the truth⋯. especially considering his real father is the one who got my wife into drinking. Last I heard, he died of Cirrhosis, so I figured⋯. hell, I'm his father now. No sense in being honest about it."

Silence then hung thick in the room. He

finally turned to her. She had tears rolling down her face. "You⋯." she muttered.

He gazed at her. "You now know the truth my dear⋯. And you must realize⋯.. we can't go on like this. I want you to help me."

She shook her head, getting up. "No⋯. *You* are not my father! I don't know who the hell you are, but you're not him! My father wouldn't lie to me and treat me the way you just did!!! And⋯. what you've done to Greg??? I can't forgive you, and I sure as hell won't help you!!" Elissa had screamed out at him in anger, but was shaking visibly in fear too, backing away from him towards the door. He wasn't worried though, because he knew what to do.

"Elissa?"

She stopped, staring at him nearly stumbling over her own feet in fear. He stepped up closer to her, and just as she tried to turn the doorknob, he shot her with a needle, hidden to the camera. She started blinking rapidly, losing her balance.

"Everything that just happened here has gone out in a live video stream over your website⋯You're over my dear⋯. We both are⋯."

Kay Romano lit the last candle in the front room, blowing out the match she had used and throwing it away.

"Ok···. That' s the last candle, " she went on, looking out the window as the rain splattered against it. She sat in the armchair beside her husband Steve who had been very quiet. "Steve? You ok?" she finally asked.

He sighed, closing his eyes in hesitation. He knew he had to tell her, considering God only knew where Tom was. "Kay···. You know how Dr. Harner has been gone for a while now, " he went on. "And···. you also know about the drug shortages we' ve been having in the hospital. "

She nodded. "Yeah Steve···. it' s been all over the news, thanks to his daughter. "

Steve had to smile in spite of himself. Funny how everything always turned back to Elissa lately. Then suddenly as if realizing what he was about to tell her, he went back on track, serious again, as lightning illuminated the room.

"Well···.. I know exactly who is responsible for it. And the reason I know this is···. " he paused before going on, knowing this was it. She' d probably ask for a divorce after this. "I was in the storage room when the person came down to take the stuff···. They caught me screwing one of the interns, and said if I told anyone, they' d say they caught me cheating on you···" he went on, his lower lip shaking. "I' m···.. so sorry hon···. "

A very loud clap of thunder sounded, knocking the power out at Peter's hotel. Monica had been sitting there in total shocked silence after he confessed the truth to her.

"Monica?" Peter finally managed out.

It remained silent. A brief flicker of lightning illuminated her face though, to reveal tears flowing down it.

"Oh geez…. Monica, I know I should have came forward sooner, but with everything else your family had been through…and I'm still reeling from my mom's death," he went on, after a pause.

"Besides, would you have actually believed me?"

There was no response. Peter put his hands up to his head. "Jesus…. Monica, what do you want me to say?"

Finally she softly answered him. "There's nothing to say…. We need to have blood tests run, find out the truth."

"But blood tests WERE run…. That's how my mom found out Monica. She was devastated. They ran the tests before they found the cancer-"

"Which…. is probably why she was trying so hard to contact me," she went on, sadly. "My God Peter…. All this, it-literally changes everything."

He nodded. "I know."

She shook her head. "What on earth do we do about this?"

He gazed at her. "As soon as you feel you're ready···.we face it···"

Kayla was more than halfway through the book when she heard the loud crashing sound from downstairs. She was already on edge from what she was reading in the book, and what she found downstairs freaked her out even more.

The tree from the front yard had apparently been struck, because part of it had come through the front room window, bringing with it a fried electrical wire tangled in it's limbs, already burning them. Kayla stood there looking at it in horror for only a few moments, before running to the phone···.

Greg was looking over the contents of the envelope with the flashlight that was unfortunately starting to go dead···.with horror filling him. He heard his cell phone start ringing and reached for it.

"Hello?"

Kayla was on the other end, freaking out and

he could hear sirens in the distance. She kept cutting in and out but Greg got, "through window" "fire", and "help me".

"I'm on my way." he told her, jumping up. He dropped the envelope, and its' contents on the floor in the process, and just stared down at them as if they were foreign to him. He shook his head, and hurried out not even bothering to shut his dad's door behind him this time….

This time he used the excuse he was taking Elissa to the hospital as he left the hotel. He set her in his backseat, knowing she wouldn't be conscious for several hours. Which was good. It gave him time to think of what to do next. He had not planned this far, simply because he thought Elissa wouldn't act like this….. a spoiled brat. This was not the daughter he raised.

He floored through a yellow light before it turned red. Her website got over a million hits a week. So, it was probably now well known about Monica…Greg…. Kayla…Seth…everything. He thought he had covered things well, even for his partner's sake. Steve's marriage would be saved now, but his wouldn't. He was asking Monica for a divorce. As soon as he figured how to do away with Elissa.

He winced, as tears entered his eyes. He really didn' t want to. But she was never going to love him like he wanted her to. He thought destroying Mark would be the answer to all his problems. He could come here, get his little girl back and she' d agree to hide away with him. She' d get plastic surgery, become someone new, just like he had. No one would ever suspect a thing.

He made a sharp right turn at the next corner. But as her father he would never force her into something like that. No, there was only one option left for the both of them now.

He hit the accelerator with his foot, flooring it as he headed to his and Elissa' s final   destination⋯.

Chapter 15

Monica went to the window of the room to gaze out into the stormy darkness. Peter had gone to the bathroom. Tears blinded her vision and blended in with the stream of rain falling down the window.

She was still reeling from what Peter had revealed to her. Her whole life had been a lie. Everything surrounding her was not what it had seemed. She felt angry, stunned, relieved, and sad all at once.

"Monica…"

She turned to face Peter as the lightning illuminated his face.

"Did you want to stay here? It's late and the weather is pretty nasty."

She blinked, debating it as her mind was still reeling. With a slight nod at last, she replied.

"Uhhh…. Yeah. I'll stay…"

John went to bed that night, but between the

ongoing storm and what he had saw still lingering heavy on his mind, he couldn't sleep. He finally gave up, getting up to pull on some jeans and a sweatshirt to rush out in the rain.

The guy who couldn't give a name, but an item belonging to Elissa Harner herself, had told him the hotel where he was staying at. It was too late to bother his boss now. This guy was all he had.

He grabbed his girlfriend's laptop, hoping she wouldn't mind as he left with it…..

Elissa slumped in the backseat, still unconscious as her father made a sharp right turn onto a side road.

He had this place picked out already, without realizing it. He had seen it as he flew over on Steve's bi-plane. A high cliff in an area of dense foliage…. away from society and overlooking a river rushing over rocks. He had even went there before checking into the hotel, just to contemplate everything.

He pulled into a hidden area off the road and stopped. He turned to the seat beside him, where the web camera sat. It would be pointless out here. No one else needed to see any more of this. It was over.

He got out of the car, going around to the back to pick up Elissa's limp unconscious body and carry it into the dense forest···.

Greg had the wipers on full blast, as lightning flickered every few minutes. Driving was very treacherous. Luckily, Celia's place wasn't too far.

As soon as he saw what had happened, he panicked. Luckily the rain was pelting so much, the fire from the downed power line was diminished. Even so, he wasted no time rushing around to the back door. Of course, it was locked. He bolted around to the side, desperately looking for another way in.

He could hear sirens in the distance. Good. Hopefully they were coming here. He returned to the front again, and getting brave, he lifted a part of the fallen tree that wasn't on fire, trying to move it. It was still hot though, and it burned his hands.

"Shit!!" he screamed out, after letting go of it. Apparently the rain hadn't put out the heat of the singed limbs enough. He grasped his reddened soaked hands, which had some black ash on them now too, mixed with dirt.

"Greg!" He heard Kayla's voice cry out, as

he looked up. Apparently what he had managed to move, was enough to make a path to the door. Ignoring his hands for the time being, he dashed for the door⋯.

Monica had gone into the bathroom to shower after Peter offered her some of his own clothes. He sat down, realizing the storm seemed to be tapering off somewhat. There was still lightning but the rain had let up, and he couldn' t hear it slamming against the window as hard.

He kicked off his shoes and sat back, just as there was a knock at the door. With a look of confusion he got up to answer it. Before him stood the reporter he' d spoken to earlier, soaking wet and holding a black bag.

"I have nothing to talk about right now," he said, starting to close the door but not before John stopped him.

"Well, I have something to talk to you about⋯. It may be life or death for Elissa Harner," he went on. "So I suggest you let me in⋯"

Kayla could see Greg from where she stood

upstairs. He'd hurt himself too, she heard him cry out. She gulped as tears started to burn her eyes. Or maybe it was from the smoke seeping through her door. She coughed, and realized with horror…. she may have to jump out the window.

She blinked, wiping her eyes as she made her way over to the window to attempt to open it. It went up just as she heard Greg's voice…..right behind her.

"Kayla don't. I'm here."

The first speck of dawn was slowly stretching across the sky, by the time he made it to the perfect spot. He let Elissa down slowly in the brush. He then sat across from her on a rock, the sound of the waves below crashing gently, settling in the air. He gazed above at the spotted parts of sky that showed through the trees.

He couldn't have picked a better place to say their final good-byes.

"No! It won't come to that. She'll agree to the plan! She has to!" A voice inside his head kept insisting.

He closed his eyes as the wind picked up, and he thought he heard Elissa moan slightly…

Kayla broke down upon seeing Greg, and started to hug him but he grabbed her hand instead, leading her out of there as quickly as he could···. just as the fire department met them at the door.

"Anyone else in the house?" a fireman asked.

"Oh my God···. their dog!" Kayla cried.

As if being paged, a bark was heard as the little dog came trotting down the stairs. Kayla called it, and picked it up, hurrying from the house with Greg.

They reached the car, and got in as Greg sat there trying to compose himself. He held his hands in pain as Kayla gazed at him in worry.

"Want me to drive?" she asked.

He sighed, looking at her. "In this weather? You sure you can handle it?"

"Greg, your hands are injured. I have to drive."

He hesitated, closing his eyes and undoing the seatbelt to get out and switch seats with Kayla. Before getting in the driver's seat, she put the dog in the back.

"I hope that dog's housebroken," Greg said, as they drove off···..

Kevin blinked sleepily, as he slowly started to awaken. Light shone in the room, causing him to squint. He sat up, looking around as he wiped his eyes. He wasn't in his room. This room was much smaller.

He looked at the bed beside him, where Tina lied. He blinked, then shot up out of bed. He was naked. She was naked. And Elissa was nowhere around.

He quickly found his clothes and threw them on, leaving the room. He made his way to the room he and Elissa shared, unlocking it. He came in, and stopped dead in his tracks. Elissa wasn't in the room, but it was apparent there was a scuffle. Elissa's purse was over in the corner, her phone lying beside it, facing up. There was a missed call on it.

But Kevin's attention was focused on what he had nearly stepped on as he came into the room. He kneeled down, picking up the syringe to a shot needle….

Peter took a deep breath, as John made his way past him, into the room. He took out what was in the black bag, a laptop, as he asked Peter where there was an outlet in the room.

He shook his head. "Mind telling me what this is about first?"

John sighed, heavily. "There may not be any time···. My girlfriend thought it was nothing more than a publicity stunt, but I just don't know···."

"Publicity stunt? What are you talking about?" he asked quizzically.

John rolled his eyes. "Elissa's site···. it has a live stream on there of this guy, claiming to be her father and acting rough with her. I couldn't see much more, because the power went out." he went on. "But something about it just put me on alert. I'm trained to watch out for certain shit, I am a reporter after all."

Peter stood there, his blood running cold.

"I figured···. since you obviously have some sort of connection to Elissa, which you're not willing to share···that you should know,"

Peter looked down, holding the back of his neck.

"So, who are you? Really? Are you part of this? Is this a scam? Is she really in danger, can you help her?"

Peter took a hand over his face, releasing a deep breath. "There is no scam. And I can well assure you, whatever this is, I am NOT a part of."

John shook his head. "Then who the hell are

you? How did you get that locket of Elissa's?"

"I'm her brother!" he finally blurted out, stunning John. "Everything else is a really long story, but-I'm her real honest to God brother…..Ok?"

Chapter 16

Elissa moaned again, moving more. She felt incredibly lightheaded, and weird···.like she was in a fog. She opened her eyes and blinked.

The sun shone bright in her face. She had to wince, as she tried to get up. Another wave of dizziness swept over her. What was wrong? The last thing she remembered was being in the hotel room, arguing with her father···.. *her father!*

She started to panic, looking up. She could now see where she was, the scenery at least. It was a beautiful area. She struggled to sit up more, trying to see if her father was around. She spotted him several feet away, leaning over and doing something, with his back to her.

She blinked, thinking she could escape if she was smart···.if she could fight her way through whatever she had drugged her with. Her mother a druggie?! He had real nerve. HE was the druggie. He was definetly not the man she had known and loved as her father for years···.

She took a deep shaky breath, trying to get up carefully and quietly. The whole time she watched her father, to make sure his focus wasn' t on her. What was he doing anyways?

She was finally up on both feet, although extremely shaky. She tried to take a step only to lose her balance. She stumbled back into the brush, precariously coming close to the edge of the precipice. She gasped out loud, looking down over it to see stories and stories of pointy rocks leading down to a rushing river.

Her father jumped up, hearing and seeing her, and rushed over to help her up. "You' re not wanting to leave me yet, and start without me dear, are you?"

She gasped, trying to scoot away from him. He smiled at her shaking his head. "It' s ok my dear. Everything' s going to be all right⋯" he went on. "Very soon⋯"

Monica had gotten out of the shower, taking her hand across the mirror clearing some steam off of it, and gazing at her watery reflection. She put the t-shirt and lounge pants on that Peter⋯. her son⋯. had given her to wear. She smiled, looking at the pants which had tiny beer mugs on them, along with the Budweiser logo, and the t-shirt which had printed on it *My Bad Ass T-shirt*.

She sighed, taking her hands through her wet tousled hair. She did need to at least try to call Greg from there, and tell him she was ok. He'd be worried sick in this weather. Although he'd wonder why she was with Peter. He was Mark's friend. She could fill him in with the rest later.

She turned to leave the bathroom, to see if she could make the call now⋯that the storm seemed to be subsiding⋯.

Kayla came to the end of the street, stopping at a red light⋯.that was blinking.

"Looks like the power must be coming back," Greg said, looking up as she made a right turn.

She glanced at his hands. "How are your hands?" she asked.

He looked down at them. "I think they're going to be fine. Definetely got some blisters forming though," he replied, letting out a low whistle, holding them, and looking at her. "How are you? Ok?"

She reluctantly sighed, and turned to him nodding. "Yeah. I think so."

He gazed at her for a while, then his gaze went down. "I need to call Elissa. Let's see if the cell lines are back up." He took out his cell phone carefully with his hands as he tried her number again. It began ringing instantly. "Good. It's ringing." he told Kayla, as he waited for someone to pick up…

Kevin was kneeled on the hotel room floor, gazing at the syringe trying to process why it was there, as worry coursed through him. That's when the familiar tune of Elissa's cell phone started up and he looked over at it, only for a suspecting second before getting up to answer it.

"Hello?" he said cautiously.

"Kevin? Where's Elissa?" Greg's voice asked in his ear.

He looked around the room, back at the floor where the syringe lied. Worry flickered through his eyes.

"Kevin? Where is she? I called earlier, and got dead air after someone picked up…"

He put a hand to his forehead. "Oh my God…"

John stood there, mouth open, his expression one of contorted bewilderment.

"You' re⋯.. her–brother? She has another brother?"

That' s when they heard the bathroom door open, and Monica stepped out.

"No⋯Elissa had only one brother. It' s a really long story–"

"Who are you? What' s going on?" Monica asked.

John turned to her, putting out his hand. "Hello Ma' am⋯.. I' m John Keller, a reporter for Channel Four news. I' m here on important business concerning Elissa Harner."

She blinked, and turned to Peter. "I' m her mother. What' s going on now?"

John glanced at Peter who just looked at him, with his head lowered, from underneath lowered eyebrows.

"Maybe⋯. you' d both better have a seat. We have a lot to discuss⋯."

Elissa looked at him, her breath coming in ragged gasps.

"Dad⋯.. don' t do this. You need help ok? But not the type I can give you," she went on, pleadingly. "Can we just drop this, and go home? I promise you, I' ll get you the help you need."

He stared at her, the smile disappearing.

"We're not going back there. That's not the place for us Elissa."

She shook her head, distraught fully griting her teeth. "It's where our family has been all these years,"

"What family? Elissa, we aren't a family! Think about it···I had to live under a made up fictional name, as a LIE with you and your mom···.hell I even had to lie to Greg, make him think *I*

was his father! Don't get me wrong, when I first met your mother···.as Seth Brewster, then as Tom Harner, everything was great. But now···.do you honestly think we can get that back? Think about it Elissa···.*you're* even a fake. Your legal last name is Harner, and it's all a joke. In fact, I bet your chat rooms and message boards are lighting up right now···about what a fake you are···"

"You asshole!" she screamed at him, and he slapped her hard across the face.

"Shut up! I was hoping Hollywood hadn't changed you, but apparently it did···" he got up, his voice and face faltering. "I loved you Elissa, I truly LOVED you. I wanted to set things right, but···.now, I just want to get this over with. The quicker I do, the less drawn out and painful it will be,"

He turned and went back over to where he had

been working on something, as Elissa scrambled up and tried to run. But the drug in her system had not totally worn off yet, remnants of it slowing her down.

Next thing she knew she felt something trip her from below···.a string of some kind. She cried out, as she felt herself going down, and being dragged backwards as she screamed out, trying to grab hold onto other stuff···eventually giving up and crying defeatedly···.

Meanwhile, miles away Celia sat in front of a computer, checking e-mail messages. She was signed up to receive updates on Elissa's site, and went into it···to see the video stream going on still. It had been set to continiously repeat itself.

She sat there watching it in sheer confusion and horror. "Hey mom! Come here and look at this!"

After a few minutes, she came in tired looking, as she stood behind her daughter. "What is that?"

"That's Elissa, and···I think that's Kayla's dad. But···.look what he's doing to her···"

Her mother shook her head, her mouth dropping open. "I don't believe this," she said.

Celia shook her head. "Neither do I···I think I' d better call Kayla···"

John showed Monica and Peter the video feed after getting the laptop set up. Monica stood there, putting a hand to her mouth and nearly breaking down.

"Oh my God···. It' s···. Tom!"

Peter looked at her, then back to the monitor as the drama unfolded. They watched···and listened to the whole grotesque display, till the very end. Monica was in tears, as John closed the laptop. Peter just stood there, his mouth partially open, in awkward shock not knowing what to say or do.

"What did he do to her?" Monica asked. "We have to call the police, I-Oh my God···. My baby!" She broke down, and that prompted Peter to put a comforting arm around her. He stared at John.

"You' re with the media···. you can get the cops on this quick," he said. "We' ll tell you everything, give you first rights to the story if you get the authorities on this···pronto···."

Greg' s heart skipped a beat.

"Kevin? What the hell is going on with

Elissa?"

After a long moment Kevin's voice came back on, shakily. "I don't know Greg···. I-just got up here. I was out late···. working on the movie," he said the last part oddly···. oddly enough for Greg to know he was lying.

Greg let out a staggered breath, creasing his eyebrows. "You don't know where she is? Yet you have her cell phone···. hmm, gotta tell ya Kevin, I don't know about this."

There was a brief moment of silence before Kevin spoke again. "I'm being honest Greg. I just fucking got here. What is your problem anyway?"

"My problem is you! Elissa's been through hell the past month, and you built her hopes up for this stupid trip thinking you two might actually spend some time together! And now, she may be hurt somewhere thanks to you!"

He hung up angrily, not even giving Kevin a chance to respond.

"What's going on?" Kayla asked, worry edging her voice.

Greg closed his eyes, trying to compose himself. Anger and worry were boiling inside of him right now. "Take me to the airport Kayla,"

"But-"

"Kayla, just take me to the airport···. now," he went on. "I have to find out what's happened to Elissa···"

Elissa was at the edge of the precipice, now crying softly in hysteria. She was totally bound, and now she knew what her father had been doing. He was making an anchor in the ground to throw her off the precipice by···. he was going to actually hang her, it appeared. Kill her.

He tightened the straps on the anchor he'd made. "Ok···. Looks good." he smiled, getting up and heading over to Elissa. "Aw now, Elissa···This isn't going to be so bad as you think···After this, you don't have to worry about a thing. No more contract hassles, crazy fans···brothers wanting to write books about you," he went on. "It's going to be wonderful···. you'll see."

She stared at him. "Please···. I am begging you. I'll do anything you want. I'm your baby girl, your princess, remember?"

He blinked, and Elissa thought she detected some hesitation. Some flicker of emotion.

"Daddy please···. I know you're there, this is not you. Where's the guy who used to hug me every day, the one who always was there for me when I needed someone to sit by my bedside after a bad dream, or help me with a school project?"

He looked down. The whole time Elissa had

been silently and discreetly working to free her hands.

"I love you daddy⋯. you' re so important to me. Always there for me, when I wrecked my bicycle, or my stereo broke⋯. All the wonderful holidays we spent together, when you bought me my first car for Christmas, the year I turned 16. ⋯How can you put an end to all this?"

He closed his eyes, and a sad expression donned his face. Elissa could feel the straps loosen and finally become free. She kept on going though, feeling more hope as she did.

"Daddy? Please⋯. I love you. I don' t want to lose y-"

"Elissa⋯. Stop. Enough. This⋯has to be done, it' s the only answer. You' re only making this harder. "

He started to grab her but she was quicker. She had stalled enough for the drug in the shot to wear off and felt more energy. She surprised him, and he looked at her with wide shocked eyes as he flailed back.

"Daddy? Daddy no!" she screamed, realizing she had actually pushed him, not shocked him so much. He stumbled backwards over the short edge as she screamed out, and cried. She tried to step forward, but part of the rock she stood on was crumbling and before she could move much further it gave way, as she screamed⋯.

Chapter 17

Officer Sidney Ryman was lying back in his bed, having fallen asleep mere minutes ago, when his bedside table phone rang. He jolted up from a sound sleep, and fumbled for the phone, putting it to his ear.

"' Ello?"

"Sid, I' m real sorry to bother you at home, but you' re the best person I knew to call."

He blinked, sitting up. "What' s going on John?"

He took a deep breath on his end. "We need to trace where a web cam is being filmed at, hack the site and get in there. We have a possible celebrity abduction going on."

"Celebrity abduction? Who?"

"Elissa Harner."

"Aw geez⋯." he went on, slapping a hand to his forehead. "John, are you sure?"

"Yes, Sidney I'm serious! I'm standing right here with her mother and brother and we watched the vid-"

"Her *brother*?" he interrupted.

"Yes! I'll explain more later, but this is something we need to get on now…..before it's too late…."

Kayla made a turn to head to the airport only to see the exit was blocked for constuction.

"Fuck!" she heard Greg mutter.

She quickly looked at him, finding a spot to turn around. "Is there another way to the airport?" she asked.

"Yes, but it's much longer. But I don't have much choice. God, I want to kill that Kevin…"

She hit the accelerator, moving in front of a car that honked. "Sorry!" she cried, as the car moved around her, the woman in the passenger side yelling something out at her, that sounded like, "Stupid bitch!"

Greg shook his head. "Ignore it, Kayla. Turn down here and go right."

She did as he said, glancing down at the gas tank. The arrow was perilously close to E.

"Um…. Did you know you need to get gas?"

He sighed, glancing over. "Just stop up here at the Gas Mart. I'll charge some."

He dug out his wallet, reaching for his credit card when he saw it…..and it caused him to stop. A family picture of Monica, he, his dad, and Elissa & Kayla. It was taken the year Elissa entered high school, and he had been a sophomore. He gazed at it and closed his eyes. He could feel tears welling up, and his heart was wrenching, but he couldn't cry….not now.

"Nice picture isn't it?" he heard Kayla say, as he looked at her. Her eyes were teary too. "Too bad it's not true…"

After throwing Elissa's phone down, Kevin stormed out and down to the front desk. The young girl cheerfully smiled at him from behind it. "Hi. What can I do for you sir?"

"I'm Kevin Lytle, staying up in room 311.….I'm looking for my girlfriend Elissa Harner,"

Her eyes lit up. "Elissa Harner is staying here? Oh my God, I'm like a huge fan of hers!"

Kevin closed his eyes, and shook his head. "Will you just get a manager please?"

"Sure…. just hold on a minute," she said, perkily picking up the phone beside her to page

156

the manager on duty···.

In the meantime, Tina was just waking up and rolling over onto the opposite side of the bed···.where Kevin had been···.yawning. Upon not feeling another warm body beside her, she opened her eyes.

She sat up sleepily, looking around. He was in the shower. That was it! She bounded out of bed, still naked, hoping to surprise him in the shower.

But she stopped, holding back the curtain not seeing him there either. She turned around with a disgruntled frown of confusion.

The man she had met last night at the bar···.before Kevin made it in···.had told her he'd pay her a thousand bucks, if she'd keep her producer busy that night···.with a flirtatious wink, saying "If you know what I mean." Hard to pass up. She would have led Kevin up to her hotel room and fucked him with or without the thousand bucks···.but it was still pretty cool anyways.

She wandered back into the other room, smiling as she slipped a robe on and leaned over, getting into her purse, pulling out the bundle of cash···..

Pebbles and rocks, along with other debris fell off skimming the side of the long cliff. Elissa hung perilously by the very device her father had intended to kill her with. She gripped it tightly with her hands, taking in fearful gasps as she stole a glance down at the rushing water before her···. where her father lied across a large rock awkwardly, face up with blood running down his forehead···. and his eyes wide open. He stared lifelessly back at her, his mouth still open in an O of shock.

She broke down crying, turning away and grasping the rope tighter. It was ironic···. the very thing her father had intended to kill her with···had saved her. Upon losing her footing and nearly falling she had instinctively grabbed the rope. It had appeared, dangling before her like a lifeline.

She sobbed and gulped, biting her lip and closing her eyes. She couldn' t look down anymore. That was for sure.

She set her forehead against the rope, fending off more tears unsuccessfully···..

Monica and Peter gazed back expectantly at

John as he ended his call. He gave them an affirmative nod. "It's getting taken care of. Sidney's off duty right now but he's going to jump on it. He's our best hacker around. He'll get answers fast, and get right back with us."

Peter raised one eyebrow. "A policeman who hacks?"

John looked at him. "Yeah⋯. How do you think they bust internet shit? Not by simple browsing, I tell you."

Monica spoke then. "So⋯. they'll be able to find my daughter?"

John gazed back at her reassuringly. "Yes, ma'am. They'll track her down and everything. And since you told me she's supposed to be in The Virgin Islands right now, that's a huge help to start out with,"

Peter nodded, then touched Monica's arm briefly. "Hey, I think the storm has lit up. Didn't you need to call Greg?"

She nodded quickly, going over to the phone to dial⋯.

Twenty minutes later, Greg and Kayla were in the airport terminal waiting on a flight that would take him to The Virgin Islands. Everything remained silent between them.

Greg was first to finally speak. "Kayla···. I'm sorry."

She kept her gaze down and shook her head. "None of this is your fault."

He looked down. "Maybe···.that other part isn't true. It is fiction···.the work of a seriously delusional person."

"It seems to add up doesn't it? Gil, the stepbrother to Elizabeth finds out in the end he's no more related to his father than Elizabeth," she went on. "And···.I'm sorry, but···.I've never really been able to see you and Elissa as brother and sister···.I liked it with me, but···.she adored you in school until she found out mom was marrying—"

"The man who I believed was my father." Greg finished for her, staring off into space and finally shaking his head. He rubbed his forehead soothingly.

Kayla bit her lip. "I'm starting to wish I'd never read that stupid book. It's torn our family apart."

Greg looked at her. "No, no Kayla. It hasn't. My feelings for you, Elissa, and Monica haven't changed."

"But the family *has* changed Greg. I don't have a brother···.maybe not even a father," she said, her voice cracking.

He stared back at her as his flight was

announced. "That's me, sis. I have to-"

"I'm *not* your sister…. Just don't call me that ok?" she said, tearfully.

His heart began wrenching. And perhaps now, for the first time he thought sadly…. he realized how much he adored not just Kayla…. but Elissa and his stepmother as well. He gave her a warm embrace which she didn't fight off until his flight was announced for the last time.

"Go…Just go. Get on that plane. Go save my sister. OK?"

He let go of her, sincerely praying he'd be able to bring Elissa back to her…. safe and sound.

Kayla kept her head down as he left, until her phone rang. She quickly got it out of her purse, glancing at the caller ID screen to see Celia's cell number coming up….

Monica shook her head as she let the phone ring on the other end, finally getting voicemail on the fourth ring. "He's not picking up," she murmured to Peter and John. But they were talking to each other, not even paying attention. After the tone, she spoke into the phone.

"Greg…. it's me, Monica. Just wanted to let you know I'm all right. I'm at the Hosterman Hotel with an old friend of Mark's…. I hope everything's all right there. Please call me as soon as you get in. The number is 555-7318,"

She hung the phone up, wringing her hands together. She really hoped Greg was ok, and hadn't ended up in an accident in this weather trying to look for her. That was all she needed now, two kids to be in danger.

She winced, closing her eyes distraughtfully…..

It was already mid afternoon there in The Virgin Islands as the plane landed. Greg got off the plane, and called every hotel in the area, asking for Kevin and Elissa's room, posing as a creative consultant for the movie that had "misplaced" their hotel and room number, and couldn't get through on Mr. Lytle's cell.

On the fifth call, he hit pay dirt. A perky girl, who couldn't have been much older than Elissa piped up at the mention of his name. She generously gave him the room number, gushing about what a big fan she was of his clients'. He handled the girl as patiently as he could, expediently getting into a cab he hailed, telling the driver where to go as he snapped his phone shut….

Elissa's arms were starting to hurt, and her palms were sweaty making her slip every now and then as she struggled to keep hold of the rope. She was desperately trying to hang on, wincing as the rope cut into her hands. They had to be bleeding. Her throat hurt from screaming out so long.

The sun was starting to dip behind the cliff, so it was anyone's guess how long she'd been hanging there. She felt herself slip again and she tried to pull herself up, as she felt and heard more rocks and debris falling.

"No!" she feebly called, trying to raise herself up with gritted teeth. That's when she felt herself go down more·····..the entire rope did. She gasped, seeing that the rope was coming undone at the top.

With an incredible pounding of her heart, she realized she would HAVE to pull herself up if she expected to get through this. And she *had* to····.it didn't seem like anyone else was going to come help her. She couldn't believe no sightseers or anyone had heard her. Her father had apparently picked a perfect spot for them to be alone. She shuddered at the thought of him.

The rope started to come undone, tearing more. She gasped aloud, and started to try to pull herself up, and that's when she heard it. She thought she was imagining it until she saw Greg standing at the top of the cliff.

"Elissa! Hang on!!" he cried out.

She gasped, crying out again, as the rope tore more…. only what seemed like a few threads remained there now. "Hurry!" she called out hoarsely. He probably hadn't even heard her.

The next thing she knew, another rope was being thrown down beside her. She glanced at it, hearing Greg's voice.

"Get a hold of the other rope Elissa! I'm going to pull you up!"

She did as he said, although shakily, and still almost losing her grip and falling. She felt herself being pulled up slowly until she was right at Greg's feet. She put her arms around him, wobbly and crying hysterically.

"It's ok. Everything's ok now." he soothed her.

After a long while, she faced him as he still held onto her, keeping her steady. She felt like a shaky rag doll in his hands.

"Greg, dad's dead…I killed him! I didn't mean to, but—"

"It's ok Elissa. I know you didn't. The authorities are on their way, they will handle everything." he said, even then the sound of sirens audible in the distance.

She sniffed, shaking her head. "How did you find me? I had been yelling forever, and⋯I honestly thought I was going to die," she said, her voice breaking.

"I went to your hotel, and spoke with security . We watched video of the hotel, in your hall and I identified dad of course, carrying you in and out. They got the car and the plates on camera from the parking lot surveillance. They called the police, giving them the car make and plate numbers, informing them of the situation, but I couldn't just sit around⋯.I had to find you."

She gazed at him, and for the first time felt like the moment between them was way beyond intimate and she wanted to kiss him, the way deep in her heart⋯.in a part she had long ago buried⋯.she wanted to. Instead she felt her knees wobble and she fell against him weakly.

"Come on," he coaxed her, guiding her away from   the   cliff⋯..164

A preview of the next book in the Celebrity Secrets Series:

Kayla stood in the living room back at their house, where the police had just given them the official ok to go back in and resume their lives. Like *that* would happen. Monica gazed at her youngest daughter with an expression of anticipation and regret.

"And….**that's** what happened. So, as it turns out Mark was never actually your real brother."

Kayla looked down.

"Kayla? You ok?" her mother went on. "I know, it's quite a shock…..but it all makes such perfect sense!"

Kayla shook her head. "No it doesn't. It just makes perfect sense to you because it makes everything easier," she went on, muttering to herself. "The book never said anything about this."

Monica's expression turned disgruntled. "It *does* make sense Kayla. And what do you mean, the book never said anything about it?"

Kayla took a deep breath, but couldn't say anything more, as there was a knock at the door.